Trusting Again

Book 4 in the Second Chances series

Peggy Bird, author of *Beginning Again*,
Loving Again, and *Together Again*

C R I M S O N
R O M A N C E
F+W Media, Inc.

This edition published by
Crimson Romance
an imprint of F+W Media, Inc.
10151 Carver Road, Suite 200
Blue Ash, Ohio 45242
www.crimsonromance.com

For Anita, Beryl, Ruthann, and our handsome date at the Heathman who made the opening scene of this book easy to write.

Chapter 1

"I love it when she has the men in the audience sing the chorus to 'Eight Miles Wide,'" Liz Fairchild said. "Hearing deep voices sing about the size of their vaginas never fails to amuse me."

Cynthia Blaine had known Liz for years and, although she wasn't surprised by anything the other woman said, she was sometimes still astonished by where Liz chose to say it. However, shushing her was a waste of effort. So was pointing out the startled expressions of the people who'd heard the comment. Liz had never learned to care about keeping her voice down or her opinion to herself.

"You like saying that out loud, don't you?" Cynthia said.

"No one objects to that word anymore, do they? And if they do, maybe it'll clear out the place so we can get a table. Otherwise, we're out of luck. The bar's full," Liz said.

They'd just come from a matinee of the Oregon Symphony featuring Storm Large, a performer with a great voice and an amazing repertoire of songs, not all of which were appropriate for the faint of heart, a category which included Liz's favorite, her signature song. Now, standing at the entrance to the Heathman Hotel bar, the women were hoping to find a table so they could have a glass of wine.

This girls' afternoon out also included Amanda St. Claire, who was doing a recon for a table in the back. Amanda hadn't been out much since the birth of her baby and Liz, whose art gallery exhibited both Amanda's art glass and Cynthia's designer jewelry, had, as she described it, "arranged the excursion to rectify that."

Amanda rejoined them just in time to catch the last part of the conversation. "It's full there, too," she said waving toward the other room. "There are three empty chairs at a table for four, but there was a guy sitting there. I guess he's waiting for people to join him."

"Did you ask?" Liz said.

"No, it seemed rude."

"If he has the only empty chairs in the place, it's not rude. If you can't do it, I will." Liz headed to the area that served as overflow bar, tearoom, and place to lunch for the hotel restaurant.

In a few minutes, she reappeared in the door to the back room and motioned to the other two to join her.

"Oh, my God. Did we get lucky," she said in a low voice. "And not just by scoring a table. The man we'll be sitting with is one of the most beautiful creatures ever to walk the planet."

"So, Liz, when did you say Collins will be back in Portland?" Amanda asked, trailing behind Cynthia.

"I didn't and you're usually more subtle than that. I love Collins but I'm not blind. You'll understand when you see this man," Liz said. "And to answer your question, however rhetorical it may have been, this is his week in Portland. He should be home now. With any luck, he'll even have dinner—"

"Holy hell." Cynthia stopped so suddenly, Amanda ran into the back of her. "Is that the guy you're talking about?" She nodded toward a man sitting alone at a table for four, a glass of red wine in his hand.

"Yup, isn't he gorgeous?" Liz asked.

"I know him," Cynthia said. "He commissioned a piece of my jewelry a month or so ago for his girlfriend."

"Damn. There goes my plan to set you up. I figured I might find a way for Amanda and me to leave without you so he'd ask you to dinner."

"Don't you dare do anything like that," Cynthia said, raising her voice slightly and emphasizing the "dare" part of the sentence. The last thing she needed was Liz's heavy-handed matchmaking. It was uncomfortable enough when Liz tried to fix her up with one of her artists. Cynthia definitely didn't want any attempts to get her together with this man.

Not when he woke up a hatch of butterflies in her stomach every time she thought about him. Ever since he'd walked into the Erickson Gallery, she'd been full of fluttery things on a regular basis. As she was now.

She smoothed the skirt of her plain lavender linen maxi dress, trying to get rid of the wrinkles, then tied the ends of the deep purple shrug she wore over it a little tighter around her waist. It was too late to wish she'd worn something sexier. Or had put her tawny blonde hair up in some intricate roll, rather than a simple braid down the middle of her back. Worn fuck-me shoes instead of the flat sandals she had on. Put on a little more make-up; put on any make-up at all.

Oh, for God's sake. Wearing something else wouldn't have made any difference. He has a girlfriend. One he spent big bucks on for a birthday present. And what the hell was she thinking, anyway? Even if he wasn't attached, he was way out of her league. After the whole Josh disaster last year, she'd vowed never to get herself in a similar situation again. She'd barely gotten out of that relationship with any shred of ego intact.

As the three women approached the table, the subject of her fantasies stood to greet them. Cynthia was sure his picture was in the dictionary next to the phrase "tall, dark, and handsome." Cliché it may be but, in his case, true. He was well over six feet tall, with skin the color of a latte, and thick, black-brown hair that curled around his ears and at the back of his neck. The first time she'd seen him in Seattle, she'd immediately wanted to thread her fingers through that hair. Lick up the side of his neck until she got to his jaw line, an earlobe, his full-lipped mouth, whatever she could reach to kiss. Put her arms over those broad shoulders. Earn one of those sensuous smiles.

Everything about the man was burned into her brain including what was, she was pretty sure from watching it walk away from her, the best ass in the Northwest. So she knew if she wasn't careful, before this little unexpected encounter in Portland had ended, she'd likely be drooling all over him like a St. Bernard.

When the man recognized Cynthia, a broad grin spread over his face and lit up his brown eyes. "If I'd known you were one of the women who were table-less, I'd have carried it out to you. With a bottle of champagne."

"So, the birthday gift was a success," Cynthia said.

"Absolutely," he said. "It was the hit of the evening. I've been out of town on business or I would have let you know how much my friend appreciated it." He turned the smile on the other two women. "Sorry. Didn't mean to be rude. I'm Marius Hernandez. Cynthia created an amazing piece of jewelry for me to give a friend as a birthday present."

"This is Liz Fairchild, Marius. She has a gallery in Portland where I have some of my work. And this is Amanda St. Claire. She shows her work at The Fairchild, too."

"Everyone knows Amanda St. Claire's art glass. And I've read about your gallery, Liz. I don't know what I've done to deserve the pleasure of three beautiful and talented women joining me but whatever it was, I hope I do it often." He gestured toward the table. "Please. Sit. Let me flag down a server and get you something to drink."

Liz took the chair next to Marius and Amanda sat opposite her, leaving the place across from him for Cynthia. She moved the chair back from the table a bit, sure that if he went back to the slouch he'd been in before he stood, she'd be brushing knees with him and she didn't think she could handle that.

But instead of inhabiting the chair with a casual sprawl, he sat up straighter, his forearms on the table in front of him which put her hands, not her knees, in danger. Even without touching him, Cynthia was unnerved by being this close to him. She played with the strap of the shoulder bag in her lap, twisting her fingers in it, trying not to watch him. But she wasn't able to keep herself from sneaking peeks at him out of the corner of her eye.

"Cyn, what do you want?" Amanda's voice broke through the heated mist that had obscured every other thought as soon as she'd seen Marius. "We've ordered our drinks and some food to share. The server's waiting for you."

"Sorry, a glass of house red, please."

"Make that a bottle of the Malbec I'm drinking," Marius said to the server before asking Cynthia, "Is that okay with you? I'm drinking red wine, too, and with you and Liz ordering red, it makes sense to have a bottle."

"I've never had a Malbec," she said, "but sure. Sounds fine."

"Most Northwesterners who drink red wine stick to local pinot noirs. But this is one of my favorites. It's from Argentina, from a high altitude vineyard in the Andes. I think you'll like it."

"So, Marius, now that we have that settled," Liz began, clearly finished with the wine discussion, "I'd love to know more about you. You commissioned a piece from Cynthia in Seattle, but are hanging out in Portland. Do you live in Washington or Oregon? Or do you slide back and forth across the Columbia at will?"

He seemed to take Liz in stride, merely smiling at her as he answered. "I live in Seattle. I'm in Portland for a coffee convention."

"There are conventions for coffee?" Liz said. "Who knew?"

"Coffee's big business. Especially now that Starbucks has taken it out of the supermarket and made it gourmet. My family has been in the business for several generations and we've seen the change. Benefited from it, to be honest."

"You sell coffee?" Liz asked.

"Not in the sense I think you mean. We're brokers for coffee plantation owners in Central America. We arrange the deals between coffee roasters here and plantations there."

"Coffee roasters like Starbucks?"

"Don't I wish. No, we have several dozen clients in and around Portland, same in Seattle, and a growing number in California."

"Is your family in Seattle?" Amanda asked.

"Miami. My family came from Cuba when Castro took over." Before Liz could ask another question, he went on, "My grandfather started the business. My father and uncles run it now and my brother, a cousin, and I are next in line. I was sent to Seattle to open a West Coast office to handle all the business your coffee culture was bringing us. It's only me, a couple computers, and an assistant but..." His self-deprecating smile didn't really match the rest of his confident body language.

Which was what Cynthia was staring at—his body. Especially his shoulders. His gorgeous shoulders were clad in a jacket that never wrinkled when he moved, like it was part of his skin. She was sure he had his suits made for him. The one he wore today was brown, the perfect complement to his milky-coffee skin. The fabric looked expensive, imported from someplace like Italy. His cream-colored shirt had French cuffs held together with chunky gold cuff links. She wanted to touch the fabric of the shirt; it looked so soft, so smooth. Maybe it was silk, like his tie, which she thought was Prada.

What the hell was wrong with her? First obsessing about her clothes, now his? What men wore had never been of any interest to her. Women's clothes barely held her attention for more than the ten minutes it took for her to throw on jeans and a T-shirt every morning. She had to pull herself together. Liz and Amanda were having a normal conversation with this man while she sat like a lump, too busy thinking about things like his clothes—or what was under them—to say anything, much less anything intelligent.

"I guess you must find Seattle a bit of a change from Miami," Amanda was saying when Cynthia tuned back into the conversation.

"You have no idea. Just about everything's different, from the weather to people's idea of fun to the politics. I've gotten to like it now. Except for the beaches. Even after two years, I still miss Florida beaches."

The wine arrived; he tasted and approved it. The conversation went on, mostly around Cynthia not with her. She'd made some progress toward normalcy—she'd stopped obsessing about his clothes. Now, she was intent on making sure no part of her body touched any part of his. When he handed her a glass of wine, she took it without coming in contact with his hand. She kept her knees clenched tightly together and primly set to the side of her chair so there was no chance they would brush his. She avoided eye contact.

But the one thing she couldn't get away from was the smell of his aftershave or cologne or, who knows, maybe pheromones, wafting across the table. He smelled like some exotic spice she couldn't name. She had never, in her entire life, smelled anything that good. It was irresistible. Like every other part of him was, from the crown of his head to the just-got-out-of-bed dark stubble on his cheeks and jaw that would feel wonderfully scratchy on her skin. From the body under that custom-made suit she'd stopped thinking about until now, when she started thinking about it again, to his voice that was like a good piece of music, deep and resonant, layered with meaning. And his eyes, oh God, his eyes ...

"Cyn, is something wrong? You're so quiet." Amanda sounded concerned.

Before she could answer, Cynthia caught the expression on Marius's face. Damn. He knew exactly why she was quiet, why she was sitting like some well-behaved schoolgirl. It seemed those brown eyes could see into her heart and soul.

"I was thinking about a new piece I'm working on. Sorry."

He raised an eyebrow and buried his half-smile in his glass of wine.

"Is this for my gallery or are you going to waste it on that place in Seattle where you still have your work?" Liz asked.

"It's a commission that came from Max's gallery, that place where the owner has been as good to me in Seattle as you've been to me in Portland. And didn't I just bring you my Victorian neckpieces no one else has seen?"

"I guess I'll take that as some sort of atonement for giving him your Cleopatra collars first. Not that anyone in Seattle would ever appreciate anything like that."

A Cleopatra collar was exactly what Marius had commissioned from her, but demonstrating he was as smart as he was sexy, he only winked at her and stayed out of the discussion.

The conversation moved on to subjects less likely to make her discomfited. In response to his questions, Amanda explained to Marius some of the fine points of kiln-formed glass art. In return, he answered hers about coffee buying. In her usual outrageously flirty manner, Liz encouraged him to come to her gallery before he returned to Seattle. Cynthia said little unless prompted by her friends and even then made only brief comments, still tongue-tied by sitting across from him.

An hour later, Marius glanced at an expensive-looking watch, re-buttoned the top button of his shirt, tightened his tie and apologized for having to leave for a business dinner. Before he left, he shook the hand of each of the three women, seeming to linger with Cynthia longer than with the other two. At least it felt like he lingered, taking her smaller hand between both of his, holding it in what felt more like the clasp of a lover's hand than a good-bye handshake. She noticed, as she had when they first met, that in spite of the beautiful clothes, he had calluses on his hands that could only come from some kind of physical work. It added an aspect to him that fascinated her even more.

She hoped he hadn't noticed how her hand trembled when he held it.

• • •

Marius couldn't believe his luck. He'd been trying to find a way to get back to the Erickson Gallery for weeks so he could do what he should have done when he'd picked up the gift for a family friend—ask the beautiful artist who'd made the piece to have dinner with him. But he'd been traveling on business for most of the past month, ending up in Portland, where he'd been bored and counting the days until he could get back to Seattle.

Until he decided to kill time before his dinner meeting with a glass of wine. And there she was.

In only two brief encounters, Cynthia Blaine had managed to intrigue him. Curvy where most of the women he'd met lately had been long and lean, her face was clean of make-up, her eyes clear of calculation about what his net worth might be. He had his pick of arm candy, but going to dinner with women who were conventionally beautiful, fashionably dressed, and often more ambitious than he was—which was saying quite a lot—had worn thin. Not that he was looking for a long-term commitment. But someone real seemed like a nice change. And Cynthia Blaine was that—real and talented and beautiful.

When he'd first met her, he'd thought she was equally attracted. But he had wondered if she'd written him off because he was obviously buying a piece of expensive jewelry for a woman even though he kept emphasizing it was for a *friend*, hoping she'd get the inference. Today he thought the message must have gotten through. The way she'd flushed when he smiled at her, held her body back from touching him, looked away so he wouldn't know she'd been staring at him all seemed to say she felt the same attraction.

What he hadn't been able to do was cut her out of her herd of friends without being too obvious or obnoxious. So, he scribbled a note on the back of a business card and left it with the server when he had the bill for the women's drinks charged to his room. She assured him she'd get it to the woman in the purple dress with the long braid.

•••

Marius was barely out the door before Liz turned on her friend.

"Cynthia, what the hell is wrong with you? Why didn't you tell us about him?"

"Why would I tell you about him? He was just another customer," she replied. "Can I have the last bit of that cheese?" She reached for the plate. Liz pushed it out of her reach.

"Don't change the subject. How could you not think we'd be interested in one of the most handsome men ever put on this earth?"

"Don't be ridiculous." She tried for the cheese plate again. And failed, thanks to Liz's determination. "I just sold him a neckpiece for his girlfriend."

"The girlfriend part, I grant you, is a shame. But, my God, girl, just run down the list of the other virtues: killer good-looking, charming, polite, interested in what we have to say, willing to ignore phone calls while he talked to us, the good taste and money to commission work from you and buy that suit. What's not worth talking about on that list?"

"I guess I wasn't paying attention."

Liz snorted. "Right. You were stunned into silence just sitting across from him."

"No, I wasn't."

"Don't bother, petal. No one will believe you. It was too obvious. Not that I blame you. You could drown in those eyes. And his smile gave me some idea of what it'll feel like when I get old enough to have hot flashes." She fanned herself to make her point more obvious.

"Did you notice his hands?" Amanda asked. "I love the way he talks with them. They're so big and graceful. I bet he could palm a basketball with them."

Cynthia's hand was still trembling from the handshake. Oh, yeah, she'd noticed his hands all right.

"A basketball? Honey, he could palm anything I have with them," Liz said. As the other two women burst into giggles, she added, "Please don't repeat that in front of Collins. He doesn't have much of a sense of humor when I make comments like that."

A half hour later, Liz went to pay the bill and learned that Marius had taken care of it, adding one more item to her list of reasons Marius Hernandez was God's gift to the world. The three women parted at the parking garage across the street from the concert venue, Liz headed for Southwest Portland where the man she lived with waited; Amanda to Northeast Portland, her husband and her new baby, and Cynthia for the freeway back to Seattle.

• • •

The dinner hostess at the Heathman always rearranged the desk to suit the way she liked things before she started her shift. Tonight, while she was moving things around, she found a business card with a note written on the back. No one seemed to know who it was for or why it was there. She pitched it into the recycling.

Chapter 2

Cynthia happily pointed her car north on I-5 even though she knew she probably faced heavy traffic going home. For once, she was looking forward to dealing with it, hopeful that concentrating on the traffic would take her mind off the subject of Marius Hernandez.

It didn't happen. Once again, the mental tape of the day he'd come into the Erickson Gallery switched on in her head. And she was there all over again.

* * *

She was wire-wrapping a bead when the bell on the door rang, indicating someone had come into the gallery. Looking up, she was so distracted by the gorgeous man walking toward her that she poked herself with the silver wire she was using, drawing blood. That's how she greeted him, sucking on her finger to make it stop bleeding.

He removed the sunglasses she couldn't imagine he needed in March in Seattle, took command of her gaze with his espresso brown eyes, smiled and said, "I'm looking for Cynthia Blaine. That wouldn't be you, by any chance, would it?"

The smile alone made her knees wobble. Add the brown eyes and handsome face and she wasn't sure she could trust herself to speak. So she just nodded.

"I'm Marius Hernandez." He put out his hand to her.

She took it after wiping her hand off on a wet rag to get rid of the blood and saliva and trying to alter what she was afraid was the expression of some teen-aged groupie who'd run into Justin Bieber. His big hand enveloped hers, making her wish the handshake could last for hours, maybe days.

"I'm looking for a specific piece of your work. For a gift."

Please, God. Make it a gift for his mother, his niece, a sister. Anyone but a wife.

"I have a friend who's about to celebrate a significant birthday," he continued, "and I want to give her the necklace she admired when she was in here recently."

Damn it, a her. Nice going, God. Technically you gave me what I asked for—he isn't buying it for his wife. Remind me to be more specific next time when I ask you for something.

"Tell me what the piece looks like," she said.

"A big necklace. It looked like a collar, she said. Four or five inches wide. Fastens in the back. Silver wire with crystals and rubies woven into it. My friend said it looked like something a princess would wear."

"Ah, my favorite Cleopatra collar. It just sold a couple days ago."

"Can you make another just like it?"

"Actually, I don't make duplicates. But I have one I'm working on with clear glass and pearly glass beads that's similar. Might that work?"

"Glass? I thought—she thought—my *friend* thought—they were gems."

"Nope, all glass. Here, let me show you the piece I'm talking about."

He loved the piece and didn't argue about the price. After leaving his business card with his email and office phone number so she could call him when it was ready, he left.

She stood staring at the card for a few minutes. The sale was great, but knowing where to contact him wasn't going to do her much good personally. Not when he was spending serious money on a girlfriend's birthday present. With a sigh, she went back to her wire wrapping. That old saw was right. All the good ones are taken.

• • •

Her mental tape of their first meeting lasted just long enough for her to miss the exit for Centralia, where she always stopped for coffee. Reluctantly, she faced reality: Marius was going to be with her every mile of the way. In the inevitable gridlock at the damned Tacoma Dome curves, he was actually helpful. She spent the time crawling through traffic trying to identify what made him smell so good. It made being stuck there almost tolerable.

Eventually, she got to the Ballard neighborhood where she lived, but she didn't lose him there, either. After she turned off the ignition and pulled her duffle bag from the trunk, Imaginary Marius walked with her into her apartment and watched her unpack and set up the coffee maker for the next morning. Then he followed her to her bedroom, a sexy smile on his face while he watched her undress. He even managed to crawl into her head while she slept, spending the night in her dreams where he also crawled into her bed.

• • •

She was more successful blocking him from her thoughts over the next month. Most of the time. Except when she was drinking coffee. Or a glass of Malbec with her dinner. It wasn't the one he'd bought—she couldn't afford that one. But she found the names of a couple more reasonably priced vintages online and hunted them down. He was right. She liked it.

Fortunately, when she was in her studio he was mostly absent. So she made sure she was in her studio every hour she could be. It was easy enough to do. The half dozen galleries up and down the I-5 corridor and on the coast where her work was placed had, for the past eighteen months, been bringing her both a steady flow of sales from pieces she consigned there and from commissioned work. Her income was close to stable for the first time in her career as an artist.

Ever since budget cuts had eliminated her job as a middle-school art teacher, she'd supported herself with as many as three part-time jobs at once and her art. Gradually, as she became more successful at the latter, she'd been able to quit her job at the restaurant, giving her more studio time with only three or four shifts at the Erickson Gallery and an occasional weekend day at the bookstore to supplement her income. It was a modest living, but she didn't have particularly expensive habits.

Her growing success had one consequence she hadn't expected. A write-up in the newspaper about her Cleopatra collars had brought her to the attention of several non-profits in Seattle looking for a donation for their fundraising auctions. Most of them she turned down for lack of work to give them. But a couple months ago, a friend who staffed the committee for Pacific Northwest Ballet's annual auction happened to call when she'd had a collar returned from a gallery on the coast. She agreed to donate it. In exchange, she was comped a ticket for the cocktail party and auction.

Under most circumstances, she wouldn't have gone. She hardly had the kind of money it took to bid on any of the items in the auction even if she'd wanted to. And she didn't exactly run in the social circles of the people likely to be there. But three things made this event tempting. First, it was taking place at the Olympic

Sculpture Park, one of her favorite places in the city, where huge pieces of work by famous sculptors sat outdoors with Elliott Bay in the background.

Second, Liz had hinted in a recent phone conversation that she and Collins might be in Seattle for the auction. Liz loved events like that and Collins needed to be in the city to check on the progress of a piece of his work that was being installed in the park. So Cynthia RSVP'd "yes." Even after Liz emailed that their schedule was getting crazy and they might not make it, she didn't change her mind. By then, the auction catalog had arrived and the third reason kicked in: Marius's company was listed as a sponsor of the fundraiser.

In her fantasies of what his life was like, she saw him attending events like this one, wearing an Armani tux, handing a crystal flute of champagne to a stunning-looking woman who was wearing a beautiful ball gown and an only-too-familiar Cleopatra collar. Why she wanted to torture herself by seeing him like that, she couldn't explain. But she wanted to see him again, even if he was with someone else.

This time, on the off chance she'd run into him, she was more careful about what she chose to wear. Not that there was a huge inventory from which to select. She'd never been much of a clotheshorse and, given her limited budget, that was a good thing. There was only one thing in her closet she thought would work—her summer gallery-opening dress. It was pale green pseudo-silk and had spaghetti straps that did little more than fall off her shoulders at inopportune moments. But the dress was form-fitting and did just fine with non-functional straps. With it she always wore her favorite knock-off designer sandals with four-inch heels and only enough gold leather to keep them on her feet and anchored to her legs.

Because she liked the way it made her neck look long and graceful, she took the time to get her hair twisted into a semi-braided up-do. To wear with her favorite gold earrings, she'd brought home from her studio a recently finished neckpiece with handmade beads in aventurine green glass decorated with gold leaf. She knew she would eventually sell it, but she loved it so much she wanted to wear it once before putting it in a gallery. Marketing, she called it.

When she was ready, she treated herself to a cab so she wouldn't have to hassle with parking, and she was off to the sculpture park.

The indoor area where the auction and cocktail party were being held was jammed with people. While waiting for her nametag at the registration table, she looked around at the crowd. Other than the president of the ballet and her friend Jasmine, who was frantically dealing with both registration and the last minute details of the auction, she didn't recognize anyone. No Liz. No Collins. No…no anyone.

Jasmine hugged her when she got to the head of the registration line. "I'm so glad you're here. I know you'll have a great time. I've seated you over on the other side of the room with the other artists."

"Is there anyone here, other than you, I'll know?"

"You know Spence and Doug, don't you? They're over there. Spence donated one of his paintings. And Janet Bracken's there, too. She has a lovely piece of pottery in the auction."

Jasmine handed Cynthia her nametag and directed her to the wine and her table. *Jas was right,* Cynthia thought, when Spence gave her a huge kiss and hug as soon as he saw her. *Knowing Spence, he'll flirt with me all evening even with his husband Doug sitting beside him. This could be fun. Even if I don't see…him…see Liz. I meant see Liz.*

The wine was decent, the appetizers enough to count as a modest dinner. The conversation among the group of artists was fun. Eventually, the president of the ballet made a pitch for the upcoming season, introduced a brief performance by some of the company's dancers and brought on the auctioneer for the main event of the evening.

The auction went very well. At least, it seemed to Cynthia it did. The bidding for every item was lively; for her piece, even heated. In the end, someone she couldn't see in the crowd bought it for three times what it would have sold for in one of her galleries. She was happy for the ballet, but wondered if this meant she should raise her prices.

After several rounds of bidding interspersed with breaks for refills of wine and the occasional raffle, the event ended and the crowd began to thin out. She had no more reason to stay, but before she called a cab to take her home, she decided to have a quick wander around the grounds outside.

• • •

Marius had originally declined the invitation extended to him as a sponsor of the ballet's fundraising event. After being out of town for weeks on business, the last thing he wanted to do was attend a charity auction. Then the auction catalog arrived. Cynthia's name and a description of the Cleopatra collar she'd donated made him change his mind.

She'd ignored the note he'd left for her at the Heathman and he didn't know why. He'd been sure the right signals had been there that day in Portland. She was as aware of the attraction between them as he was. He wanted to find out why the hell she hadn't acted on it. It bothered him not to know. Although he hadn't seen a ring of any kind on her left hand, he supposed it was possible she was married or engaged. Maybe had a boyfriend or was living with someone. Whatever the reason, he wanted to know. Since it was possible she'd be at the auction, he retracted his "no" and accepted the invitation.

But once he got to the event, he discovered he had a minder, a ballet board member whose job it was to make sure he had a pleasant evening at a table with the other sponsors and board members. There was no chance to wander around, to see if Cynthia was there. A few minutes before the auction began, he finally spied her across the room and was disappointed to see she seemed to be with a date. At least, the man sitting next to her acted like a date, his arm around the back of her chair, leaning in and whispering to her.

He sat through the auction trying to come up with a way to talk to her. She didn't look in his direction, not even when he bid on her donation. Damn it to hell, nothing was working out. And now the event was over and he'd lost his chance.

Wait. She was leaving, going out to the sculpture garden, alone, leaving the man who looked like her date deep in conversation with another man. He made his excuses to the people at his table and headed across the room toward the same door, tracking her every step.

Mother of God, she was beautiful. Tonight, she was dressed in something pale green that hugged her body, exactly as he wanted to. Her tawny blonde hair was twisted up on her head in an intricate-looking set of braids and knots. His fingers itched to unpin it, slowly pull the braids apart, as he kissed her neck and shoulders. He was sure her hair felt like silk, sure her skin was soft and tasted sweet.

She was exquisite. Cool and reserved-looking at first glance, the intensity he'd seen in her sapphire blue eyes when he'd talked to her in the gallery made him sure she would be anything but reticent for the right man. A man like him. He planned to find out as soon as possible if he was right.

• • •

She was standing in front of her favorite piece, the huge Oldenburg typewriter eraser, when she heard, "How many years do you think it'll it be before they'll have to explain what a typewriter is, much less a typewriter eraser?"

Even if she hadn't recognized the deep rumble of his voice, she would have known the exotic smell of his aftershave anyplace. Marius had been there after all.

She'd gotten what she'd hoped for, but her racing heartbeat reminded her what effect he had on her. Now that it was too late, she remembered how tongue-tied he made her. A deep breath was necessary before she faced him. A couple of deep breaths, actually. Then she turned to see that amazing face and those eyes, warm with…with what?

She stuttered out, "Oh, hello. Yeah…ah…I guess you're right. It'll be like…maybe like…Renaissance paintings…all the references to saints. Uneducated peasants knew the symbolism. We don't…have to have…you know…a guidebook."

He pointed at the sculpture as he walked closer. "You're not comparing those of us who know what that is to peasants, are you?" he teased.

She could feel her face redden. "Of course not." If she was reading him right, he was enjoying her discomfort.

"No, I guess you weren't because that would include you, since you recognize it. I bet you could even write the guidebook entry about it." He was standing so close she swore she could feel the heat from his body on her bare arm. "So how would you explain it, if you had to?"

She tried to put words together that made sense. "Well, let's see…uh, maybe something like…something like it was used with a typewriter, the precursor to the computer." She turned back to look at the sculpture and the words came more smoothly now that she wasn't looking at him.

"Then, I'd explain that Oldenburg wanted people to look differently at everyday objects, like erasers and clothespins. But maybe someday they'll claim he meant for the typewriter eraser to be symbolic of the ease with which we erase our past, forget everything that has gone on before and tie that in with forgetting what a typewriter is." When she was finished, she faced him again. She stifled a moan in the back of her throat when she saw the sensual smile that warmed his eyes and her insides.

"Nice. Not only can you write the guidebook now but you can also predict the guidebook of the future. Maybe you've discovered a new career path for yourself."

"Thanks, but I'll stick to my jewelry." She glanced down at her feet, then back up. "I didn't see you and your friend earlier."

"My friend?" He looked genuinely puzzled at her comment.

"The one you bought the birthday present for."

"Ah, that one. She's not the kind of friend it sounds like you think she is. The birthday gift was from my family, not from me. Her family and mine go way back. So, no friend tonight. Or any night, for that matter."

She was relieved but he was the one who looked it.

"Is that why you didn't call me?" he said.

"I don't usually call men out of the blue."

"Even if the man leaves a note asking you to call?"

"What note? What are you talking about?"

"I left a business card with my cell number on it with the hostess at the Heathman asking you to call me if you'd like to have coffee or a glass of wine."

He didn't have a girlfriend. He was there alone. He'd left her his phone number and asked her to call. "I never got it," she said. "If I had, I would have called if only to thank you for paying for our wine that day."

As if swooning with pleasure, the wayward strap on her dress slipped off her shoulder and fell down her arm. He took the one step he needed to close the gap between them and slid his forefinger under the strap, slowly moving it up her arm to where it belonged, his finger creating goose bumps where he touched her. He patted the thin piece of fabric into place before stroking down her back to her waist, where he kept his hand.

"Wouldn't want you to have a wardrobe malfunction," he said.

The pressure of his touch, the heat of his hand, made her shiver, made her nipples contract into tight buds, her back arch ever so slightly in his direction. She was sure he heard her sharp intake of breath trying to get enough oxygen to her brain to cool her whirling senses.

"Are you cold?" Before she could stutter out an answer, he slipped off his jacket and draped it around her. "The breeze off the water can be chilly in the evening."

As if it was the night air making her shudder. As if he didn't know exactly what was making her tremble.

He continued, "I hope your date won't be unhappy when you go back in wearing another man's jacket. Although, it would serve him right for letting you wander out here in the chilly air all alone."

"I'm here by myself, too, and I wasn't going back in. I was saying goodbye to the sculptures before I left."

The smile became a grin. "I saw you sitting with a man at your table and thought…"

"Spence? He's an old friend who flirts with everyone, including me. But his husband Doug was there, too. So it was all quite harmless."

"I'm glad." He looked only half serious. "I mean, I wouldn't want you to get in trouble by flirting with someone who's already taken." He resettled his jacket on her shoulders. "Look, now that we've gotten it sorted out that neither one of us is attached to anyone else, would you like to have a cup of coffee with me?"

She hesitated for a few seconds, not sure she should give in to the impulse to spend more time with him. But she couldn't resist. "How can I say no? You must know all the good places for coffee. I'd love to."

"I know the best place in town. Where's your car? You can follow me."

"No car. I took a cab."

"Perfect. I'm parked in the garage under the building. But first, I have to go back inside to pick up my auction item."

"Oh? What did you bid on?"

"A Cleopatra collar for my sister. I thought if I was the successful bidder, I might have a chance to meet the artist who created it." He touched a bead on the neckpiece she was wearing, then traced his finger over the collarbone next to the bead. "But if I'd seen this first, I might have tried to get it off you." He must have noticed the startled look on her face. "Convinced you to sell it to me, I meant. My sister likes green."

Chapter 3

After he retrieved his auction item, Marius led Cynthia to the elevator and into the garage. When he punched his remote, the lights on a convertible sports car lit up. Even if she hadn't recognized the insignia, "Porsche" written across the back of it told her what kind of car it was. It looked just like the man who owned it, dark and sleek and very, very sexy, exactly what she would have imagined he'd drive, if she'd thought about it.

"It's beautiful," she said as she slid onto the leather seat.

"She is, isn't she?" he said. "My family gave it to me as a birthday present when they sent me out here. They thought I deserved a consolation prize for having to leave Miami."

"It never occurred to me that anyone would be unhappy about moving to Seattle. Did you really hate the idea so much you thought you deserved a present?" She was sure she sounded defensive about the city she loved.

"At first, I admit I did. I didn't want to move. But I've discovered there are definite charms to the Northwest." He put the key in the ignition. "Is it okay that the top's down? I don't want you to be too chilly."

"Not a problem. It's such a beautiful evening. And I have your jacket to keep me warm."

"You're right. It is a beautiful evening," he said. "Let's take the long way around to coffee and find a place to look at what first convinced me I could like the Northwest."

When they arrived at Discovery Park, he offered his arm to her so she could navigate the uneven ground in her sandals. They walked out to a good vantage point for watching the water. They stopped and she immediately unhooked her arm, uneasy at the feel of him against the side of her breast, at her hand holding so tightly to him. She thought she saw him smile slightly, as if he knew exactly what she was doing. But he only said, "Here. This is what I fell in love with."

They watched the water for a moment or two in surprisingly comfortable silence. Finally, he said, "The water everywhere was the first thing I came to appreciate about Seattle. I sail and this is a great place for it."

"I used to sail when I was growing up and I loved it, too. But it's been a long time." Glancing over at him to see his face when he answered the question she was about to ask, she said, "What else do you like about us?"

He paused for a moment, as if he was going to answer the real question, the one that asked what he liked about her, but he answered the surface question. "Mostly the attitude people have. Everybody seems to enjoy life, to take the time to appreciate what's here. And the setting—not only the water but the mountains all around, like no place in the U.S. I've ever been."

"I can't imagine living far away from the water or the mountains. My favorite place is the perfect combination of those two things."

"And where would that be?"

"The San Juan Islands. I always think of them as a chain of drowned mountains. I could live there, I think."

"I sail there as often as I can. It's some of the best scenery around."

They walked back to the car and he headed to the Queen Anne neighborhood. He pulled into a small garage under a very modern looking house built over the side of a hill.

"This is a good place for coffee?" she asked even though she was sure she knew the answer to her question. She also knew she'd probably have said "no" if he'd immediately asked her to come home with him. But sliding into it this way made it feel all right. Somehow in only a short couple of conversations he'd made her feel at ease. When she wasn't feeling so terribly attracted to him she couldn't think straight.

"It's the best place in town. It's my home. Are you uncomfortable about being here? We could go someplace else, someplace more public, if you'd like."

"No, it's fine. It's a beautiful house. And I'm sure the coffee will match."

He opened the car door for her and preceded her up a circular staircase that went from the garage to the kitchen. After he took the jacket from her shoulders and hung it on the back of a chair, he took off his tie and unbuttoned his collar button. Saying, "Make yourself comfortable. I'll get the coffee going and join you in a few minutes," he busied himself with a canister of beans and a large machine she assumed made coffee.

She wandered out of the kitchen to look around. The house was as stunning inside as it was out. The open-plan kitchen had granite counter tops and stainless steel appliances. The living room had two glass walls; in the center of the third wall there was a floor to ceiling bookcase on which glass and pottery pieces were displayed as well as books. Interesting paintings—abstract, landscape, and portraiture—flanked the shelves.

A cozy group of chairs and love seat sat around a freestanding gas fireplace set out from the glass wall opposite the kitchen area. Hardwood floors were covered in the right places with carpets in classic designs. It was very modern yet somehow still warm, inviting, and comfortable. She was just about to sit in one of the overstuffed chairs when the view from the deck outside caught her attention.

From every angle of the deck that seemed to wrap around much of the house, there was a view of the downtown city skyline. All the iconic Seattle symbols were there—the Space Needle, Elliott

Bay, a couple of ferries, Mt. Rainier. It was the most stunning view of the city she'd ever seen from a private home.

"Oh. My. God." She apparently said it loud enough for him to hear. He came out and stood beside her, his hand over hers on the railing. She stepped away from him, trying to be casual about it.

"I had the same reaction the first time I saw the house," he said. "As soon as I saw this view, I made an offer. Didn't even ask for an inspection and never saw the bedrooms until I moved in."

"Marius, this is the most amazing…"

He traced her cheekbone with his index finger. "Say that again." His voice was warm and husky.

She moved back a step and gave him a puzzled look. "This is the most amazing…?"

"No, the first part. Say my name again."

"Why?"

"I like hearing you say it." He lifted her hand from the railing and, overcoming her initial resistance, brought it to his mouth and kissed it. "I'll like it even better when you're in my arms and say it. When you're in my bed."

She pulled her hand free of his. "What makes you think that's going to happen?" She knew her voice sounded shaky and it annoyed her.

"It won't happen tonight but eventually it will, *querida*. We both know it will. There's been something between us since the day I walked into the gallery. Something very good and very powerful."

As if to prove what he was saying, he gathered her into his arms. She knew she should probably put up at least a token resistance, but she couldn't find the will to, because he was right. There was a strong pull, a potent chemistry between them.

For weeks, she'd been thinking about what it would feel like to have his arms around her, to rest her head against his chest and listen to his heartbeat, to feel the heat of his body against hers.

She'd thought about the exotic smell of his aftershave, the warmth of his brown eyes looking into hers; she'd wondered what it would be like to kiss him.

And now he was doing what she'd fantasized, tipping her chin up, looking deep into her eyes before holding her face with one hand and kissing her.

It was so much better than anything she'd imagined. His mouth was soft and tasted vaguely of champagne. When he pressed his lips against hers, she sighed, her lips parted and she felt him pull her closer. Swallowing her sigh, he urged her lips further apart with his tongue, then set about slowly exploring one corner of her lips, then the other, then her mouth. As he skimmed his hands down her back and snugged her hips close to his, she melted into him, her arms around his neck, her fingers in his hair.

Returning the kiss, she tasted and sipped at his mouth. Her arousal was evident in the hard tips of her breasts, the growing wetness between her legs, his in the erection pressing against her. He slanted his mouth, keeping control of her lips and her body with the pressure of his mouth and hands. It was a kiss she'd only ever dreamed about.

But as she began to come up through the fog, wondering if he expected her to change her mind about whispering his name in his bed sometime in the next few hours, he broke away. He continued to hold her, kissing her hair lightly, while his breathing—and hers—returned to normal. It wasn't until she trembled that he released her.

"You're shivering again. Let's go inside." He wrapped his arm around her shoulders. "That coffee I promised should be ready by now."

She was about to say the chilly night air had made her cold. But it was a lie. She knew it and so would he.

For the rest of her visit, she managed to keep out of the range of his sensual mouth and his electrifying touch. The coffee was, of course, delicious; the conversation surprisingly normal, considering what had preceded it. She found out he was thirty-four years old, one of six children and, when he had time to train, competed in triathlons, which helped explain the fit body. He loved Latin music, spy novels, soccer, and sailing.

In return, she told him she had one sister, had lived in Washington State all her life, exercised about once every five years and only if forced to, and would turn thirty in the fall. She followed local musicians Death Cab For Cutie and still loved the now-defunct band Sleater-Kinney, read literary fiction and didn't own a TV. It seemed the only thing they had in common was their love of sailing and good coffee.

He took her home when they'd finished the coffee and conversation, but it was more the latter than the former that kept her awake that night as she added additional footage to the Marius Hernandez tribute tape she'd been playing in her head since the first time she'd met him.

Chapter 4

Marius called the next evening, and the one after. No reason. Just to talk. Cynthia had almost gotten up the nerve to invite him for dinner at her apartment when, on the third evening, he asked her to meet him on Friday at a well-known downtown restaurant, which he said was close to his office. They agreed to meet in the bar.

She left her studio earlier than usual, too antsy to focus on her work. Showered and dressed before five, she sat around her apartment for half an hour—a half-hour that dragged on for two days, in her view—until she decided traffic might be so bad that she'd better leave early for the restaurant.

Right. Why couldn't she just admit she was arriving at the restaurant early because she was too nervous to stay at home? She couldn't remember feeling like this about a dinner date before. But then, he was clearly the most attractive man who'd ever asked her out. Attractive and unsuitable. Maybe not unsuitable, unattainable. Or just plain unwise.

Like Josh.

No, not like Josh. But different from the artists she'd been with since Josh had broken up with her. Different? More like completely opposite. Actually, when she thought about it, he did have a lot in common with her ex-boyfriend. Both were high-powered businessmen, both had more money than she did, and both moved in social circles far different from hers.

That was the reason Josh had left. He said he didn't want to be tied down. But he meant tied down to her. Only a few months after he walked out of her life, he married a woman whose politically prominent family could help him with his ambitions. It was a wedding that made the news because it took place on a private island and had Bill and Melinda Gates at the top of a guest list that included most of the state's political and business elite.

Surely Marius wasn't as calculating about his life as Josh was. Not that she was going to get involved enough to find out. She'd vowed never to let her emotions get tied up with someone like Josh again. All she was doing was having dinner with Marius. Flirting a little. Enjoying his charming company.

She wasn't delusional enough to deny his attraction. That would be impossible to do, even if she wanted to. Every time she saw him—every time she thought about him—her rapid heartbeat and various tingling body parts were a reminder of how attracted she was. When she was with him, she was a moth flying near a flame—a propane torch flame. All she had to do was remember not to circle close enough to get her wings—or any other part of her—singed.

Because she knew she'd not be turning down any request to spend time with him, she also knew it would take all her concentration to keep to her plan. It wouldn't be easy. Not when a surge of desire went through her just from the smell of his amazing cologne or from the intensity of those bottomless brown eyes looking at her. Not when her insides turned to liquid from his smile or when she experienced any of the dozen other reactions she had to him. But she had to keep him from taking up residence in her heart the way he'd gotten into her head, her hormones, and her dreams. That would be a disaster.

The only saving grace was that, in the struggle to keep him from getting beyond the wall she had resolutely built around her emotions, she thought she'd get help from an unexpected source—Marius himself. If there was one thing she *was* sure of, it was that she wasn't his type any more than he was hers. It was just hormones for him, too, and he wouldn't be around long enough for her to worry about, would he? But it would be fun while it lasted. Wouldn't it?

At the restaurant, she settled onto a bar chair and ordered her usual glass of house red, hoping the wine would ease some of her anxiety and her early arrival would give her heart a chance to relax into something resembling a normal rhythm. When the bartender went off to fetch her drink, she made a few last minute adjustments to her clothes—smoothing her white handkerchief-hem skirt, centering the metal ornament on the wide, brown leather belt that showed off her trim waist, pulling the sleeves of the matching top down over her wrists, making sure the strands of her handmade beads weren't twisted. She liked what she had on, even if it wasn't exactly the business dress other women in the room were wearing.

With a sigh, she acknowledged that what she was wearing was the perfect example of the differences between them. Marius was sure to be in one of those amazing suits he wore every day in his professional life. If he kept asking her to have dinner with him at places like this, she was going to have to figure a way to buy some new clothes.

Damn.

Thinking about things like buying new clothes for dates with him was exactly what she should *not* do. It could get her into trouble financially, even with her recent successes. Counting on him to ask her out again would get her into even worse trouble emotionally.

The bartender had barely gotten the wine glass onto the napkin in front of her when she grabbed it and took a healthy sip—okay, gulp—hoping to quiet her brain before her date arrived.

•••

Marius had planned to get to the bar early so Cynthia wouldn't have to sit by herself waiting for him, but he'd gotten held up by a long, involved phone call with his father, followed by an urgent email from Honduras about his upcoming trip there. As he strode into the bar he checked his watch and was not happy to see he was bordering on being late. Damn it. He didn't want Cynthia to think he was rude or arrogant enough to make her wait. Didn't want her to believe he didn't care or worse, had blown off their date. But what he saw across the room made him stop as soon as he got inside the door to appreciate the view, even if it might make him a few minutes late.

He was sure she was unaware that most of the men in the room were checking her out. Guys there with other women glanced at her when they had the chance to do so without getting caught. Those there solo were more blatant about their interest in the cool, elegant woman in the white dress with the long braid draped over her shoulder.

She was backlit from a spot above the bar, the light picking up highlights the summer sun had put in her hair. Like a magnificent cat, she looked sleek and sexy. She wasn't fidgeting or looking around uneasily, didn't play with the cocktail napkin or fuss with the wine glass in front of her; she looked…serene, he guessed was the right word. Unlike many of the women he'd gone out with, she didn't check herself out in the mirror behind the bar every five seconds to see how she looked. Either she knew—or didn't care—that she was stunning. But she was. In fact, she was one of the most beautiful women he'd ever seen.

And she was his for the evening. If the evening went the way he'd planned, this beautiful woman could be his for the rest of the summer. That was some treat to look forward to.

• • •

She glanced up from her glass in time to see him walk—no, stride—across the room toward her, a huge smile on his face. He wasn't in a suit after all but tan trousers, a dark brown jacket, and a cream colored shirt with no tie. He was to-die-for good-looking; so handsome women in the bar followed him with their eyes to see who was lucky enough to have earned that smile.

"You look beautiful," he said as he took the seat next to her and kissed her on the cheek.

"You look pretty beautiful yourself," she responded.

"Is that how women from Seattle describe men…as beautiful?"

"I'm from Port Townsend, but I would have thought you'd have heard women describe you that way no matter where they were born."

His smile was now a little too sexy for comfort. She bet she could kiss that smug smile off his face if she put her mind to it.

What the hell? Kissing him? Where had that idea come from? That might get rid of the self-assured expression, but it could also lead to something she wasn't prepared to follow up on.

Or was she? A memory of the kiss they'd shared the last time they'd been together flitted through her mind followed by a shiver of desire that drew her nipples into hard points and shimmered through her body, catching her breath in her throat. Oh, God. What was going on here? He'd barely touched her and she all but had them in bed.

In bed? Where had *that* come from?

Thank God, the bartender interrupted. "Good evening, Mr. Hernandez. I assume you'd like your usual?" Marius nodded. The server poured a glass of the wine from the bottle he was holding before saying to Cynthia, "If I'd known who you were waiting for, miss, I'd have poured this for you, too." Her half-finished glass of wine disappeared under the bar and he brought out a clean glass into which he poured for her from the same bottle.

"Malbec, I assume?" Cynthia said.

"I'm hurt that you weren't converted by my enthusiastic endorsement in Portland." Marius covered his heart with his right hand in a mocking gesture of pain.

"I was, actually; I even bought a bottle when I came home. But I didn't think to order it tonight. Force of habit to order the house red, I guess." She took a sip of the new wine. "But this is much better, I'll admit." In a nervous gesture, she flipped her hair back behind her.

He reached over and brought the long braid back over her shoulder. Playing with the end of it, he said, "It's tempting to take this hair band off and let your braid unravel. I want to see if your hair feels like silk when I run my fingers through it."

Yanking the braid from his hand, she tossed it behind her again.

"Why do you pull away from me when I touch you?" he asked, his brown eyes somehow both curious and sensual.

"I don't." She dropped her gaze, avoiding his eyes the way she avoided his touch.

"Yes, you do." Taking her hand he began to bring it to his lips. She reflexively withdrew it from him. "See?"

She closed her eyes for a moment, not sure if she was brave enough to tell him the truth. On a deep breath, she tried. "You make me uneasy."

"That's the last thing I want to do. How? Why?" He looked genuinely surprised.

"You're—I don't know—too much."

"Too much what?"

"Too much of everything. Too handsome, too sexy, too rich, too successful, too…too Marius."

The smile reappeared, this time even more smug than before. "And yet here you are having dinner with me. Does that mean you like 'too much' even if it makes you uneasy?"

"I'd be an idiot if I tried to deny the attraction between us. Even if you do make me nervous. Even if you are out of my league."

"I'm out of *your* league? I thought beautiful, talented women had a league of their own. One the rest of us could only hope to visit occasionally and only when invited."

"Now you're making fun of me."

"I'm not. You are those things, *querida*. If anyone should be intimidated, it should be me."

She almost snorted. "I doubt that you've ever been intimidated in your life."

He shrugged his beautiful shoulders. "It takes quite a bit, but the envy of all the men in the room tonight because you're with me could do it."

The maitre'd interrupted. "Your table is ready, Mr. Hernandez, whenever you are."

"Thank you, John." Marius didn't get up, but merely finished off the wine in his glass.

"Aren't we going to follow him?"

"I know where my table is. It'll be there when you finish your wine."

"See. This is what I mean. I've never known anyone who actually had his own table at an expensive restaurant."

"Which means nothing other than I entertain people for business here often and tip well. Just like a lot of other people."

She thought about it for a moment. "When you explain it like that, I guess it doesn't mean much." She finished her wine and slid off the bar chair. "So, you eat here a lot, do you? Then you must know what's best on the menu. That'll make ordering easy."

With his hand at the small of her back, he guided her to a corner where a table was set for two with privacy guaranteed by discretely placed plants and dim lighting.

"Business dinners, huh? With this lighting? Are all your clients women?" she asked as he pulled out the chair for her.

"You found me out. I asked John to lower the lights in the corner tonight. Normally, it's considerably brighter." He didn't sit across from her but at the place immediately to her left, where she could feel his knee touch hers, his foot close to hers.

Shaking off the breathlessness that always seemed to result from his nearness, she said, "Fortunately, I won't have to ask for a flashlight to read the menu since you're going to order for us."

She was rewarded with a surprised look from him. "I wouldn't have predicted you'd let someone else order for you."

"I don't normally. But you pick great wine; you serve good coffee; you have your own table here. You'll surely do better than I would. I'd just be guessing at what's good."

"All right then, I will. You're not allergic to anything, are you?"

"No, and I like just about everything. Except lima beans. I hate lima beans." She picked up her napkin and put it on her lap. "Oh, and sweet potatoes. Don't like them either."

"Good to know. I dislike seeing my dinner companion's face puff up or turn green because I've fed her something she doesn't like or is poisonous."

"I've never thought about those possibilities before, but I'll keep them in mind the next time I have the urge to let someone else order for me. They might not be so considerate."

When the waiter arrived, Marius ordered Caesar salads, Chateaubriand for two with roasted vegetables—no lima beans or sweet potatoes, please—and a bottle of Malbec. After the server left, he said, "Their beef is the best in the city, so I thought we'd eat classic tonight instead of trendy."

"Classic is good. I wondered if you'd go all oysters and champagne."

"Am I to infer from that you think—or believe I think—one of us needs aphrodisiacs?"

She could feel her face redden. "No, I wasn't implying anything. Really."

The smile that curved up the sides of his mouth was so sensual, she felt her insides begin to melt. This man affected her more with a smile and one glance of his dangerously dark eyes than any man she'd ever known could do with considerably more contact.

"We don't need aphrodisiacs. We have all the chemistry we need without them." He took her hand and raised it to his mouth. This time, she didn't pull away. He kissed her fingers then nipped at the flesh at the base of her thumb. She shuddered and saw his dark eyes get darker.

Having proved his point, he lowered their hands to the table but didn't release her until the server brought their salads.

When her hand was free, she took a deep, calming breath so she could pick up her fork without having her hand shake. But he was not about to let her breathe easy, it seemed. She felt his knee press lightly against hers. He apparently intended to keep some part of his body in contact with hers through the whole meal.

Maybe wine would help, she thought as she took a healthy gulp, hoping it would relax her throat enough so she could swallow.

Fortunately, once the food got there, it wasn't a problem. Marius had ordered a delicious meal—the beef was tender and flavorful, the wine a perfect match and the accompanying vegetables flawlessly grilled. Somewhere in the middle of enjoying her dinner, she realized she'd gotten accustomed to the light pressure of his knee and leg against hers. She tried to convince herself it was the good food, maybe the wine, making her so comfortable. Her head was willing to listen, but not her heart.

He insisted she select dessert. She was tempted by cherries jubilee and chocolate cake, but ended up asking for a cheese plate. When the waiter left, Marius had an odd expression on his face.

"I'm sorry," she said. "Are you disappointed? Did I order something you don't like? We can call him back and change it." She began to look around for their waiter.

"No, don't." He put his hand over hers. "I'm not disappointed; I'm surprised. I thought I was the only person who could resist something sweet after a meal. You ordered exactly what I would have."

Somehow, almost three hours had slipped by while they ate and talked and laughed. She didn't realize how late it was until they walked out of the restaurant into a dusky evening.

"My car's parked that way," she said, pointing to the left.

"I'll walk with you to make sure you're all right."

"I'll be fine."

"Of course you'll be fine. I'll be with you."

"You don't have to…" she began, but she could tell from the look he gave her that she was going to have company while she walked to her car.

He put his arm around her shoulders and she found herself fighting the urge to nestle into his side and just enjoy smelling him.

"Would you like to, Cynthia?" he asked.

"I'm sorry. I wasn't paying attention."

"Should I be offended that after our first dinner together, it's so easy for your mind to wander when I'm talking to you?"

"Why don't you just repeat what you said and skip the fishing for a compliment?"

"I asked if you'd like to have coffee at my place."

She took less time to say "yes" than she had the last time he asked.

They reached her little Honda Accord and she got directions to his house from downtown. She was just about to get into her car when he took her hand. Without asking the question, she knew what he wanted. The answer was in his eyes.

Brushing a few strands of hair from her face, he bracketed her cheeks with his hands. He lowered his head so his mouth was close to hers. Closing her eyes, she braced herself for the kiss she knew was coming, the kiss she both wanted and was afraid of. But instead of pressing his mouth to hers, he only lightly touched her lips with his then whispered, "I should wait until we're not in public, but I've wanted to do this all evening."

The vibrations from his mouth coursed like electricity through her body. He held her face for a few more moments, the warmth from his breath on her mouth making her feel like she would dissolve in a wet heap at his feet.

Just when she thought he would never do it, he kissed her. But it wasn't the soft and gentle kiss she expected. It was so immediately passionate, so urgent and demanding, it felt like a train had hit her. He didn't just kiss her; he took possession of her mouth as if he never intended to give it back. All of her senses were focused on her mouth, his mouth, what he was doing with his lips, with the tip of his tongue. She should have been frightened by the intensity but she wasn't, she was aroused by it.

She didn't resist, couldn't resist, but responded as he slid his tongue around hers with a sensual roll that made her head spin. The kiss took the oxygen from her body and the stability from her legs. Her breasts tingled. She was dizzy and breathless, wanting more from him, wanting everything he could give her—his mouth, his body, more of this man.

When she slumped back against the car, he kept the length of his body in contact with hers. His hands slipped from her shoulders and slid down her sides, following the curves of her body, stopping to hold her at her waist as if he knew she was in need of his support just then; before moving to her hips, pulling her into him, moving her tighter against an erection that was, she was sure, threatening to break the zipper on those expensive-looking trousers he was wearing.

Without thinking, she moved her leg to accept him, to bring him closer to her, canting her hips to feel him pressed hard against her where a moist heat was burning. As she felt him grow harder and bigger against her, a hunger came out of nowhere, surging through her and she returned the kiss, exploring his mouth, playing with his tongue, every cell in her body responding to him.

He nibbled his way from her mouth to her cheek, to her jawline then her earlobes, licking, then kissing, the sensitive spot right behind her ear. When she moaned and rubbed her hips against his, he whispered, "*Querida*, we shouldn't be doing this on the street."

She shook her head, more to clear it than to indicate an answer. "No," she gulped in air before continuing, "you're right. We shouldn't." To her ears, her voice sounded vague and far away, like she was having an out of body experience.

As she moved away from him, she saw a sweet smile play across his mouth, watched desire flash through his eyes. He gently kissed her forehead, his hands still on her shoulders. "Shall we go to my house?"

She didn't say anything for a few moments, not sure if she wanted to change her mind or race him there. When she tried to speak, she could hear how breathless she still sounded, how high pitched her voice was. She swallowed, gave a cough or two to clear her throat—her head was a lost cause—and tried again. "Remind me how to get there?"

In spite of the two times he'd given her directions, she made three wrong turns getting to his house driving through a city she knew like she knew her own name.

Marius Hernandez, she decided, should have a warning label on his forehead: Exposure to this man can result in confusion, dizziness, and erratic behavior. Women who kiss him should not operate machinery immediately afterwards.

Chapter 5

Because of her detours, Cynthia arrived well after Marius had gotten home. As she walked through the front door he'd left open, he said, "I was beginning to think you'd changed your mind." He'd shed his jacket and, from the aroma, started the coffee brewing.

"Sorry, I got turned around and ended up going south instead of north. Must have had more wine than I thought." *Yeah, right, it was the wine,* she thought.

"That's okay. You got here just in time. Coffee's almost ready. Let's have it outside. It's always a shame to waste a nice evening—we don't have too many of them."

"Oh, you out-of-staters are always complaining about the rain. You never complain about all the lush trees and flowers we have because of it, do you?"

"No, and we don't complain about the beautiful skin the women in the Northwest seem to have because they can't bake themselves to leather in the hot sun." He opened the sliding glass door to the deck for her, a wicked smile on his face. "I'll bring the coffee out in a couple minutes."

When he returned five minutes later, she was at the railing. "I could look at your view forever."

"It's almost as beautiful as you are, *querida.*" He put two mugs of coffee down on a small side table. She saw that he'd remembered she liked cream in her coffee.

"*Querida* is such a pretty word. What does it mean?"

"Sweetheart or dear. Spanish endearments always sound pretty, I think."

He was so close to her that it was tempting to nestle into his chest. Instead she asked, "Does your family speak Spanish at home?"

"My mother does. She was born in Honduras. My father had to brush up on the language when he fell in love with her—no one in his family had spoken it regularly for a generation. My brothers and sisters and I were raised with both languages, although we mostly speak Spanglish at home. No self-respecting Spanish-speaker would claim it as their language."

He turned her around so she was facing him. "But I know the correct Spanish to describe a beautiful woman when I'm standing next to her." With the pad of his thumb he outlined her cheekbones, her eyebrows, down the crest of her nose as he said, "*Bella, preciosa, encantadora, maravillosa.* You are all those things."

The impulse to move into his arms, press her body against his, was becoming overpowering. Then he made it worse.

Taking her face in both hands, he said softly, "If I kiss you now, I won't want to let you leave tonight. You know that, don't you?"

Closing her eyes to the intensity she could see in his didn't help. She could feel his desire wash over her in waves. Barely nodding her head, she managed to get out "Uh-huh."

"So," he whispered, his mouth now almost touching hers, "shall I kiss you?"

In answer, she put her hand at the back of his neck and pulled him the few millimeters it took for his mouth to reach hers.

• • •

When he'd given in to his need to taste her, to kiss her, on the street outside the restaurant, he was sure she'd change her mind about coming to his home for coffee. Her hesitation when he'd asked the second time almost made his heart stop. But here she was. and she was kissing him just as she had before.

He was trying to keep himself under control, to go slowly but his hands seemed to have a mind of their own as they slid down her sides, stopping to graze her nipples, feeling them turn hard and pebbly with arousal. His mouth moved from lips to cheek, then to her ear, where he paused to outline the edge of it with his tongue. When he breathed on the place where he'd licked, she shivered.

Both of her arms were around his neck now, drawing him closer. Even through his shirt he could feel her nipples hard against his chest. She was returning the kiss with more passion than he thought he could bear, nipping at his mouth, exploring with her tongue, making small sounds of pleasure as his hands and mouth explored her. He was harder than he ever remembered getting, just from kissing her.

The kiss could have gone on forever, but he wanted more than that. Tonight, he wanted to find out how to get her to make more of those soft, sweet sounds in her throat that turned his cock to steel, wanted to explore every inch of her body, wanted to bury himself deep inside her and hear her call his name when she came. Tonight, he was greedy; he wanted it all.

Breaking from the kiss, he said, "Follow me."

"The coffee…" she began.

"Can wait 'til morning."

Taking her hand, he led her back into the house and down a flight of steps to his bedroom. He didn't turn on the overhead light, just one small bedside lamp before yanking back the sheet and comforter. Through it all, he kept hold of her hand, stroking her thumb with his, soothing her. She'd looked startled when she'd seen his king-size bed, as if she might be thinking she made the wrong decision.

After he'd made the bed ready for them, he embraced her and kissed her forehead. "Second thoughts, *querida*?"

She smiled. "No, why did you think…?"

"The way you look right now."

The smile became a laugh. "I'm just surprised that everything in your bedroom reminds me of coffee."

It threw him off balance. "I don't understand."

"The furniture is as dark as espresso, the comforter is the color of a latte, the chairs over there, foam on a cappuccino, the rug…"

He joined her in laughing. "I may be in the business but you're the one obsessed. I just like brown." He brought her hand up to his mouth and kissed it. "If the décor isn't too distracting, can I…? He reached around her and unfastened the band that held her braid together. When it was gone, she shook her head and he pulled some of her hair over her shoulder so he could rub it between his fingers.

"It feels like silk. Like I knew it would," he said. "And your skin," he kissed her throat as he unbuckled the belt she was wearing, "it tastes as sweet as I imagined."

The belt dropped on the floor. Then he skated his hands up her back until he got to the buttons at the neckline of her top. When they were unfastened, he took the hem of the blouse and lifted it over her head.

He wasn't surprised to see she wore a white bra with thin straps, cut low between her breasts. No lace, no tiny pink bows. Plain. But the hard diamond points of her nipples showed through and he couldn't resist taking one in his mouth, just for a moment, just to suck through the thin fabric and scrape gently with his teeth, just to make her moan. Her back arched to him, moving her breasts closer, tempting him. He unhooked the bra, slid the straps down her shoulders and threw it on the floor before giving in to his need to linger there.

On his knees, he licked and tasted, suckled and swirled his tongue over first one breast then the other before moving down to her waist. Her skirt was off next and he continued his way down with his mouth, then his fingers under the white cotton panties she still wore.

But when he gently touched her wet center, he could feel her legs begin to wobble. She objected with a groan when he stood, but when he moved her back to the bed, she fell onto it and let him take off her shoes. Clad now only in her panties, she watched as he unbuttoned his shirt, pulled it out from his trousers and dropped it on top of her clothes. When his trousers and boxer briefs were in the same pile, he started toward the bed. Her eyes had widened at the sight of the erection that was now free from his clothes. On a sharp intake of breath, she licked her lips and his cock jumped in reaction to the smoky desire in her eyes.

"Do you like what you see?" he asked.

"You have the most beautiful body I've ever seen outside a life drawing class," she said. "You could have been a model for the ancient Greeks."

He smiled at the compliment. "I bet you say that to all the naked men you see."

"Is this where you tell me you think artists have loose morals because they draw nudes?" She put out her hands and when he took them in his, pulled him into bed with her.

"No, *querida,* this is where I tell you you're as beautiful in my bed as I knew you'd be." As he talked, he played with her hair. "I've wanted you here since I met you. It was your eyes at first." He leaned in and kissed each eyelid. "Then I learned how sweet your mouth tastes." He brushed his lips over hers. "Now I know how your hair feels." Using the strand of hair he'd been fondling, he grazed her nipples, making them peak into pink pearls. "And how pretty your breasts are. How very pretty."

He bent his head and substituted his mouth for the tress of hair, his tongue circling the bud of her nipple, then his mouth sucking gently, pulling at the tender flesh. "What else will I learn about you tonight, do you think?" he asked as he moved to the other breast.

She arched towards him, putting her breasts in better position for his mouth. He followed with his hands sliding up her ribs, cupping her breasts. When he looked up at her, he saw she had her eyes closed. "Open your eyes, *querida*. I want to see them." When she did, he flicked his thumbs across her nipples, heard her draw in a deep breath, saw the desire in her eyes. Saw she wanted him as much as he wanted her.

Moving his hands down from her breasts, he hit the waistband of her panties. "You're overdressed; let's take care of that." He slipped his fingers under the elastic and tugged. She raised her hips and the panties were down her legs and onto the floor in seconds.

Her hands were trembling as she reached for him, for his penis, but he intercepted them, lacing his fingers through hers and putting their joined hands above her head. He knelt on the bed, straddling her hips, barely touching her body with his. She was restless, excited, her breath quickening.

They were both so aroused, he knew he could enter her now, could bury himself deep inside her and it would be good. But he wanted her not only wet and hungry for him, but breathless from coming and crying out his name.

"I want to find out everything you like, *mi amor*. Do everything you like." He dipped his head and ran his tongue along the edge of her ear, barely touching it. He felt her tremble. "Like that. I think you like that. And this—you like this, too." He bit gently on her ear lobe then began to lick the soft spot behind her ear. This time she moaned.

"Where else are you so sensitive?" He began to kiss his way from her ear, along her jawline to her throat, sucking on the pulse spot there before moving again down her body, between her breasts. "Here?"

She sighed. "Oh, yes."

"And here, I know." He swirled his tongue around one nipple, then the other.

Although he had her hands imprisoned above her and her legs immobile beneath him, she was restless, kept trying to move, to rub her sex against his penis, her moans now gasps as she gulped in air. She bucked her hips up harder, working for release.

"Slowly, *mi amor*, slowly." He'd reached her ribs with his kissing and knew he'd have to lower her arms to go further. He released her wrists at the same time he moved his legs to free hers. She separated her legs to give him access to the delta of tawny curls between her legs, now soaked with her arousal.

Using his fingers and his tongue, he separated her labia, hunting for the nub of her clitoris with his mouth, finding it, hearing her gasp as he twirled his tongue around it, slowly at first, then faster. When her breathing quickened again, he entered her with his fingers, caressing a place inside her so she cried out in pleasure, bringing her to the edge of orgasm.

"Oh, my God," she said. "I've never…"

He did it again. "Do you like that?"

Her response was to buck her hips up, riding his hand, rubbing against him, crying out her pleasure as she tumbled over the cliff in climax.

He moved beside her and kissed her half-closed eyes then reached across her for the drawer of the bedside table. Opening the packet he took from the drawer, he removed the condom and pressed it into her hand.

"Help me, *querida*, please?"

Her cat-stretch as she came down from her climax was so erotic, he wasn't sure he could contain himself. It was all he could do to keep from immediately burying his face in her hair and his penis in her body. Mother of God, this woman did things to him he didn't know any woman could. And she did it without seeming to know how she affected him.

She propped herself up on one elbow so she could carefully roll the condom over his erection. He watched the intent look on her face, felt the light touch of her small hands as she stroked him, felt the pressure begin to build again in his body to enter her but he gritted his teeth, willing himself to slow down his reaction, wanting to make this last as long as he could and to let her set the pace.

The condom in place, she looked up at him, her eyes bright with desire. "You're beautiful everywhere, every part of you," she said. "I could look at you all night long."

"I had something in mind other than just looking," he said.

"Oh, yes, please." She put her arms around his neck and pressed herself against him. "Yes, please."

He claimed her mouth again with his; he wanted to keep it gentle, to enjoy just a little longer the pleasure of touching her, feeling her body under his, her sweet mouth opening for him but there was no way in hell he could. His control was on a long thin string and about to give out.

And she was there, too.

"Please. I want…" She didn't finish the sentence. She didn't have to. Her body told him exactly what she wanted. She opened her legs and ground her hips up against him. Slowly, carefully, he entered her. She was tight. She was hot. He was inside her and he wondered if he'd want to be anyplace else ever again.

The long, slow, in and out rhythm quickly became harder, then faster; his breathing and hers matched the speed. He pulled back to look at her, saw the flush on her face and waited for what he wanted to hear.

"Marius!" His name came out in a whoosh of breath. "Oh, God, Marius."

There it was, what he wanted, the sound of his name on her lips as she came. He could feel her inner muscles tighten around him, rhythmically milking him as their bodies moved in sync. With one more thrust deep into her, he felt his body contract and release in a mind-blowing ejaculation.

He collapsed against her, limp and sweating. He held her until they were breathing easily, although he wasn't sure he would ever breathe easily again around this woman. He kissed her forehead before slipping out of her and out of the bed to take care of the condom. When he returned, she was curled up in a ball, a sleepy, sated expression on her face.

He drew her to him, her back to his chest, his arm around her middle. They lay together like that for a long time, saying nothing. "I could stay like this for hours," he said as he nibbled at her neck and shoulder.

"Mmm, I could, too. But I should go home before I fall asleep."

"I thought I might be able to tempt you not to fall asleep just yet. And, if I can't, convince you that you don't have to go home to fall asleep."

"You want me to stay?" She turned and looked at him, a surprised expression on her face.

"Of course, if you want to. I've only just begun to learn what I want to know about you." He pressed the beginning of another erection against her and skimmed his hand over her hip and thigh as he spoke. "And I make a very nice breakfast."

"Oh, well, if breakfast's on offer…" she said before drawing his face close to hers and kissing him.

• • •

Cynthia never needed an alarm clock to wake up, her body clock worked just fine. And the next morning was no different. She woke at her usual early hour, disoriented for a few seconds until the smell of Marius's aftershave mixed with the smell of clean sheets and sex reminded her where she was, what she'd been doing and with whom she'd been doing it.

He was still sleeping, his back to her. Stretching in the glow of an amazing night with a gorgeous man, she decided coffee in bed with him sounded like a good idea so she slipped out from under the sheet to go to his kitchen.

The clothes question arose immediately. There were too many glass walls in his house for her to wander around naked. But she didn't think she wanted to get dressed in her skirt and blouse quite yet—the skirt and blouse which were still in a heap on the floor where they'd been all night. She picked them up and hung them on the back of a chair hoping some of the wrinkles would disappear before she left. In the same pile was the shirt Marius had worn. She put that on and, in her bare feet, padded quietly out the door and up the stairs to the kitchen.

Where she found a piece of equipment she'd paid little attention to when Marius had made coffee. It was huge. Artfully made, with what she assumed were coffee trees embossed on shiny copper and silvery steel, it had more dials and gauges than the control panel of the space shuttle. She touched several of them trying to figure out where to start to get the coffee going.

"Is coffee what drove you from my bed at this ungodly hour? I should hire you. You are more obsessed with our product than anyone in my family." Marius was yawning between sentences, wearing only jeans and an overnight growth of dark stubble. And he was magnificent. Dear God, he was the most gorgeous man she'd ever seen. He made her mouth dry just looking at him.

"I was going to make some and bring it downstairs for you, but I don't have the engineering degree I need to make your coffee maker work."

He laughed. "Let me. Then we can both go back to bed." He yawned again. "Sorry. I'm not much of a morning person." His eyes did a quick scan of her body as he fiddled with a container of coffee beans and his machine. "But even in my half-awake state, I can see how beautiful you are in the morning. And you do things for that shirt I doubt the maker ever thought of. Rather than work for my company, you should model for the shirt maker. They'd sell a hell of a lot of product."

"Thank you. You're very kind," she said, before she realized how stupidly formal it sounded. It shouldn't have been awkward, not after the night they'd had, not after multiple orgasms and several rounds of the best sex she'd ever had, but it was. She felt like a kid caught sneaking around someone else's house. She was in his kitchen, wearing his shirt, playing with his coffee machine. Lusting after his body.

Looking around for a distraction, she saw what looked like nautical charts spread out on the small breakfast room table. She wandered over to the table. "I didn't notice these last night."

"No? Well, we were busy with other things." The wicked smile was back.

She ignored it. "Are you planning a trip? It looks like you're going to the San Juans."

"I am. I'm going sailing for ten days, starting next Friday."

"I'm green with envy. Is this your annual vacation or something?"

"More like 'or something.' I leave soon after the sailing trip for six weeks in Central America. I always try to have some time to myself before I go on one of these big business trips."

"Where're you going in the islands?"

"Haven't completely decided yet. Definitely a couple days on San Juan Island. I have a friend in Friday Harbor, a coffee roaster who has a special roast for me, and I like Roche Harbor too. You said you liked the San Juans. What're your favorite places?"

"Haven't been in awhile, so I don't know if things have changed, but I've always liked Orcas Island for the art galleries, And we used to bicycle on Lopez. Oh, and I like Jones Island."

"Jones? Really? I've never done more than sail past. What's there?"

"The whole island's a state park. It has nice camping sites and a quiet cove or two."

He had the coffee dripping by now and was looking at her with a thoughtful expression. "Why don't you come with me and show me?"

"Come with you? I can't do that."

"Why not?"

"It's…we haven't…I mean…"

"I promise not to chain you to an oar and force you to row across the Pacific on water and hardtack. And I'll throw in having the master cabin all to yourself if that makes the offer more appealing."

"Hardtack? Do they still make that?" She laughed. "Fear of being shanghaied isn't the problem. I just can't."

"You have other commitments. I understand."

"No, not that."

"Then what?" He shook his head. "Never mind. I'm putting you on the spot. Why don't you think about it for a couple days? I'm leaving tomorrow for a quick trip to visit some of our clients in California before I go to Central America. I'll call in a couple days and you can let me know what you decide. I can't think of anyone I'd rather have sail with me, but if you don't want to, I understand." He checked his coffeemaker. "But now, coffee's ready. And my bed is calling. Want to join me?" The look in his eyes was definitely not one that said he was going back to sleep.

Chapter 6

Cynthia spent the next few days playing "should I/shouldn't I" with herself as she tried to decide whether she'd go sailing with Marius. Ten days on a boat with him sounded glorious. And scary. Romantic. And threatening. A welcome vacation when she hadn't had one in years. A definite challenge to her determination to resist falling for the most attractive, sexiest man she'd ever met.

Why was she even considering it? She'd told herself she wouldn't get involved with someone like him again. A man who could break her heart in an instant by leaving her because she wasn't the woman he needed with him. Just like Josh had.

But Marius wasn't like Josh. He was sweet and funny. Successful and financially well-off like Josh, yes, but he'd pursued her, even after he thought she'd ignored the note he'd left for her at the Heathman. God knows he was an amazing lover. But outside of bed, what did they have in common? They lived in different worlds.

The whole time he was in California, she went back and forth about going or not going. She couldn't make up her mind. Finally, she decided she'd just say the first thing that came to her mind when he asked again. But on Tuesday night, when he called from L.A., before he could even ask she said, "What time will you pick me up on Friday?"

• • •

Surprisingly, instead of the designer jeans and Ralph Lauren polo shirt she'd imagined he'd wear, when he showed up at six A.M. on

Friday, he was in cut-offs and deck shoes with an unbuttoned blue work shirt, the shirttails of which were tied around his middle. After she stopped staring at the muscles in his chest, she saw he was sipping—maybe gulping would be a better word—from the biggest personal coffee cup she'd ever seen.

"Tired from your trip?" She gestured toward the cup.

"Not a morning person, remember? It takes this much caffeine to get me going if I have to function at this hour."

"I don't understand how you can dislike mornings. It's my favorite time of the day. Everything seems possible when I first get up. Nothing has gone wrong yet."

"Except having to leave the comfort of my bed." With one raised eyebrow and a half-smile, he handed her the coffee cup and picked up two bags of groceries and her large duffle bag. "If you can take that little duffle, my cup and whatever's in those plastic bags, we can get this out in one trip."

The Olympic Mountains to the west and Mt. Rainier to the east presided over a Northwest summer morning that would have stolen the heart of even the most determined advocate for some other part of the country. The sun was out; the sky was clear. Morning light bounced off the windows of the upper floors of downtown skyscrapers that, in the winter, were often above the city's ubiquitous low-hanging clouds. Today the buildings stood proudly visible over a city just beginning to awaken.

The top was down on the car; traffic hadn't gotten to gridlock yet. Once they were out of Seattle proper, Marius hit the gas pedal and they seemed to fly. He drove with the same relaxed skill with which he seemed to do everything and Cynthia got caught up in the enjoyment of the ride. She didn't dare look at the speedometer, but then he was the one risking the speeding ticket.

However, even the Washington State Patrol seemed under Marius Hernandez's spell this morning. They were nowhere in sight. No cops. Beautiful weather. A fast car. A handsome man.

And her Death Cab for Cutie CDs. She didn't know how the day could get much better.

They made good time getting to Anacortes where the boat was docked. That's where the day got complicated, where the consequences of her decision hit. He suggested she stow her duffle bag and some of the groceries while he went to the marina locker to get the gear stored there. As soon as she went below, she saw what she should have thought about before making a decision—the quarters in the boat were tight. Standing in the middle of the living space, a seat on either side that she knew became beds at night, she wondered if she'd made a big mistake.

Within five minutes, the whole place would smell like him. She'd be squeezing past him dozens of times a day going from the deck to the kitchen and God knows what they were going to do about sleeping arrangements. He'd said she could have the master cabin to herself but …

"The master cabin is behind you," he said, coming down from the deck. "Throw your stuff in there. It'll give you some privacy. I'm used to sleeping out here anyway."

"Oh, you've rented this boat before?"

His smile was almost shy. "I didn't rent it. My friend Enrique and I own it. It's our way to run away from work. We each have it two weeks a month."

"Then it's even more appropriate that you sleep in the master cabin. I'll sleep out here."

He picked up her duffle bag and threw it onto the bed in the cabin. "There. Done. You're in there. The captain says so."

The rest of their preparation for leaving, loading supplies and gear, went better and they were ready to motor out of the marina only a couple hours after they got there. They weren't alone on the water, by any means, but as it was a weekday, they weren't part of an armada either.

When they got to open water, they hoisted the sails. Skirting around smaller islands, looking at the homes nestled in the woods along the shore or up on a hill, hoping for an eagle or two to swoop overhead, they began to make their way in a circuitous course toward Orcas Island.

She'd somehow forgotten how free it felt to skim over the water, the sea air in her face, the boat heeling with the wind. It brought back some of her best memories of growing up. In the first two hours, she laughed more from sheer joy than she had in years. It took her less than that to decide, given her choice, she'd spend the rest of the summer sailing if she could, it didn't matter where. From watching Marius, she was pretty sure he was enjoying it as much as she was. Not to mention seeing him handle the lines, sheets, and tiller answered the question she'd had about how he got those calluses on his hands.

About halfway to their destination, as if the natural world around them wasn't providing her with enough amazing scenery, Marius made the view considerably better by taking off his blue work shirt. She didn't know if he'd worked up a sweat but she was sure she broke out in one looking at him. Those gorgeous shoulders came out in all their glory, as well as the chest she loved to nestle against, the six-pack she'd run her fingers over when they were in bed, the dark hair on his chest tapering to a thin line leading down his flat belly to …

Madness. It led to madness. If she had any chance of doing something other than lust after him all day, she had to stop thinking about what was under those cut-offs. It was bad enough worrying about whether he expected her to make the first move tonight and invite him into her cabin or if she should wait for him to ask. But obsessing about it all day would only interfere with her enjoyment of the trip. She had to focus on something other than his body and what they might be doing when the sun went down and they were tucked into the coziness of the boat.

She looked around for something, anything, to take her mind off him. There. That line. She could coil it up so neither of them would trip on it. And police up the life jackets that had slid off the seats when they'd been heeled over. That should do it.

• • •

What was going on? Up 'til two minutes ago, she'd looked so happy. Marius had been trying to come up with ways to keep that look on her face every day for the rest of the trip. She was relaxed, at ease with herself and with him. After only an hour or so, she was handling the lines and sheets with the confidence of an experienced sailor, even though she'd said she hadn't been sailing in years. She was stronger than he expected, quick on her feet, graceful at everything she did and beautiful doing it. But now she looked pensive, disturbed by something. What?

Then, just as suddenly, her expression changed back. She was engaged again, coiling a line, a happy expression on her face. He liked watching her. It took a luffing sail to remind him he'd better watch what *he* was doing and not her.

It was difficult. The wind had loosened some of the hair from her braid and the strands curled around her face and neck. He wanted to smooth them back into the braid, tuck the loose ends behind her ears after he'd rubbed their silky texture through his fingers. But he'd sworn to himself that he'd keep his hands, and every other part of his anatomy, to himself until she indicated she wanted him to do otherwise.

Not that she made it easy with what she was wearing. Those cute little white shorts were bad enough, showing off the long, lissome legs he had last seen wrapped around him in his bed. But almost as soon as they were on board, she'd taken off the prim blue and white striped shirt she had on and tied it around her waist, leaving only a black bikini top that barely contained her breasts. He remembered only too well what those breasts tasted like, how her pink nipples beaded up when he touched them, how her breasts fit perfectly in his hands as he caressed them …

Mother of God, he had to stop this. When he offered her the master cabin, he'd hoped she'd suggest they share it but she hadn't. The look of fear he'd seen on her face when he'd gone below for the first time at the marina had sobered him. He didn't think she was afraid of him, but he'd apparently underestimated her uneasiness about coming on this trip. He had to make her comfortable. Once she got comfortable, it was more likely he'd get to be that way, too. Otherwise, he was going to walk around with an aching groin for ten days.

The privacy he'd promised, she'd get, even if it meant he had to sleep in the main cabin and stare at the damn door to the master cabin all night. Which is what he imagined he'd be doing tonight. Not what he'd planned, but then half of what he'd planned with this woman hadn't gone his way so why was he surprised this trip was headed in that direction?

• • •

Mid-day they moored at East Sound on Orcas Island for lunch. Cynthia had volunteered to provide all the lunches as her contribution to the trip. Today, she served up cold chicken, a pasta salad, nectarines, and brownies. He offered a light white wine or sparkling water to accompany lunch. She picked the latter. She was not about to add alcohol to the mix of sun, wind, and Marius Hernandez's half-naked body and was relieved when he chose the same.

When they'd packed up the remains of their meal, Cynthia poked around in her small duffle bag and came up with a tube of sunscreen. "I need to put more on. Want some?"

He held out his latte-colored arm. "With this skin?"

"With any skin. You mean you don't have any sunblock on? Don't you know about the epidemic of skin cancer? Here, let me." Without thinking it through, she went behind him and began to rub lotion onto his shoulders.

It was a mistake, a very *big* mistake. The heat of his skin zinged through her fingers, up her arm, into her chest, taking up so much space in her lungs it was hard to breathe. She tried to get more oxygen in by taking deep, deep breaths, but that just meant she replaced the little air in her lungs with the exotic smell she associated with him, a scent even the sunscreen couldn't mask.

And if touching his skin wasn't bad enough, there was the feel of the muscles underneath. Oh, dear God, the muscles. Trying to distract her mind from what she was doing, she racked her brain for something to think about that wasn't related to his body. Touching his body. Massaging those muscles. Which if she didn't stop thinking about would lead to licking all the way up his spine to his neck. Where she'd nibble, until she moved to sucking on his earlobe. Or maybe sliding her hands around his waist, insinuating her fingers under the waistband of his cutoffs to follow that line of dark hair.

No! She had to do something to stop the train wreck she could see coming if she kept on thinking this way. But she couldn't help herself. She loved touching him. Loved the feel of his skin and the strength of his muscles. Remembered what it felt like to have him hold her, touch her. To feel the hardness of his body against her softness. To have all that male heat against her. Inside her.

This was getting worse by the minute. There had to be something she could do. But what? What? Wait. She'd read someplace about what men did to divert themselves from thinking about sex. What was it? Oh, right. They thought about baseball. That wasn't workable. She didn't know enough about the sport to form a coherent diversionary sentence.

Okay. What was it Liz said she'd done when she wanted to stop smoking? Oh, yeah, she'd used the idea of a mental stop sign when she got the urge to light up. Cynthia closed her eyes for a minute, pictured a huge, red stop sign on Marius's back and proceeded to blow right through it to touch the next muscle.

Then she remembered her life drawing class in college, naked bodies as art project. She'd learned all the major muscles in that class and now ran through what she could remember. Trying to think of the correct names for what she was massaging worked at first. Deltoids. Triceps. Biceps. Brachioradialis.

Arms and shoulders finished.

Then on to his back. Latissimus dorsi. Trapezius. Obliques. She was on a roll. Gluteus max…oh, shit. Don't go there. Do not go anywhere near that thought. Or that muscle.

One by one, his muscles tensed and twitched as her fingers worked the lotion into his skin as if she'd said its name out loud. Maybe she had. Or was that Marius she heard? She could have sworn she heard a soft groan as she spread the sunblock down his back to the waistband of his cutoffs. She felt like moaning herself. If she didn't finish this soon, she'd be lost.

• • •

He had about twenty seconds of control left before he'd strip her naked and thrust himself deep inside her right here on the deck in front of all the angels in heaven, a half dozen boats and whoever was watching from shore. There was only one thing to do to save her—save himself—from that.

"I think you got it all," he said. His voice, he knew, was thick, hoarse. "Let me do your back."

He grabbed the sunblock from her with a grip so tight, enough lotion squirted out to save a significant portion of the population of the state of Washington from malignant melanoma. After taking a second or two to compose himself, he began to slowly, carefully, rub the cream along her arms.

Her skin was so soft, her muscles so pliant. She pressed her arm into his hand and rotated her shoulder back towards him as he smoothed the sunscreen across her back, up her neck, under a complicated set of woven strings holding her bikini top on. Ties he would love to un-complicate, un-weave, rip through, bite off.

And she made little noises, tiny moans in the back of her throat, like the sounds she made when she was about to come. He didn't think she knew what she was doing, what it was doing to him, but he didn't stop her—didn't want to stop her. Any more than he could stop himself from thinking what it would be like to ease his fingers under the front of the top, feel her breasts, touch the nipples he was sure were in hard peaks by now.

Jesus, this wasn't any better than having her put the lotion on him. Fortunately, she turned around. "I think my back's done now."

He still had a handful of sunscreen in the palm of one hand. "How about your face?" He didn't wait for her to answer before gently massaging the lotion into her forehead, along her nose, down her cheeks to her jaw, then her neck and her chest.

His fingers were now on the rise of her breasts; all he had to do was slide down the slope to her nipple. He could see them peaked against the thin fabric of her bikini top, knew she was aroused, too. Her breathing was rapid; her face was flushed. Just another inch or two …

She grabbed the tube from him and in a raspy voice said, "Good. We're both safe now."

Like hell they were. Only an idiot would think either one of them was safe after that. And neither one of them was an idiot.

When they resumed sailing, it was awkward at first. He could see she was deliberately giving him a wide berth as she moved from one part of the boat to another. It was just as well. He hadn't recovered from the sunscreen episode, either. He'd risk cancer rather than repeat that little experience.

But within a half hour, they were back to working easily as a team. She didn't seem uncomfortable when, giving her a feel for the tiller, he put his arms around her, his hand over hers. He was grateful. At least for a few minutes, he was touching her, inhaling her peachy-sunscreen scent, feeling the tendrils of her hair whip across his chest.

They sailed for another couple of hours then headed for the marina at Deer Harbor where they were to spend the night. To celebrate their first night out, Marius had made reservations at a restaurant in town. Their table was on an outside deck where they could enjoy the long, lovely evening. The restaurant had fresh seafood and a passable wine. The place was full, so the service was slow, but that gave them more time to talk.

When the server had poured wine for both of them, Marius touched his glass to hers in a toast. "You were a great crew today. I didn't need to bring out the whips and chains once."

"Oh," she said with a devilish gleam in her eyes, "you keep whips and chains on your boat?"

"Yeah, in case I have a naughty passenger. Not that I've ever had one on board. But you never know."

"So all your passengers are well-behaved?"

"That's not it. I've always sailed alone. Except for the few times when Enrique and I have gone out together."

That seemed to stun her. "You're kidding. I'm the first?"

"The boat's called *Soledad* for a reason. I wanted it for privacy, solitude. On this trip, though, I didn't want to be alone."

"Why me? You could have asked any woman in Seattle and gotten a yes."

"Just in Seattle? I thought maybe my range might be a little wider than that."

"Marius, be serious. Why me?"

"Do you really need to ask? Isn't it obvious how attracted I am to you? Can't you feel…?"

"Now you're making me embarrassed." She played with her fork and avoided his eyes.

He watched her for a few moments. "And I don't want to make you any more uneasy than you already are. So, we'll change the subject. You said you sailed when you were a kid. I've forgotten where you said you grew up. You house must have been on the water."

"It still is. I grew up in Port Townsend. My parents moved to Bellingham a few years ago but none of us could bear to sell the house, so we rent it out. My sister talks about moving back there but she and her husband both have tenure at Wazoo, so they'll be in Pullman forever, I think."

He shook his head. "You know, that tripped me up for about a year. I got it pretty quickly that UDub was the University of Washington, but it took me a lot longer to realize that Wazoo was Washington State University and not something considerably less educational. Thank God I did okay with Huskies and Cougars."

"Which any Washingtonian will tell you are far superior mascots to those wimpy Ducks and Beavers in Oregon. And don't get me started on Trojans."

"Obviously, you didn't go to school in California or Oregon. Husky or Cougar?"

"Neither. I did go to college in Oregon—Reed College in Portland. That's how I know Amanda. We met there."

"And what is Reed College's mascot, may I ask?"

"Well, there's no *official* mascot. The unofficial mascot is a griffin. Reed's not your usual college. No griffin mascot prancing around while the Ultimate Frisbee Team competes."

"A griffin and an Ultimate Frisbee team. No wonder they turn out artists."

She laughed and started telling him stories about her years at Reed with Amanda.

Seeing the light return to those blue eyes as she talked about her college years and her friend, hearing her easy laugh made whatever discomfort he'd had on the boat through the rest of the day worthwhile. He settled back into his chair and enjoyed the perfect end to the day.

Chapter 7

After the whole sunscreen thing, Cynthia had been *very* careful about where she was in relation to where Marius was on the boat. He'd seemed more observant, too, at least for a while. Eventually, they got back into their rhythm of working together. Even the lesson on handling the tiller had gone well.

She hadn't yet solved the problem of what to do about the sleeping arrangements on the boat that night, but at least they were comfortable around each other as they sailed. More than comfortable, actually, at least on her part. She loved being with him.

Especially after the adorable thing he'd done at the marina in Deer Harbor. After they'd tied up, he'd helped her onto the dock from the boat and then casually took her hand, holding it lightly, almost shyly as they walked up the dock to get a ride to the restaurant where they were having dinner. It was sweet—puppy love sweet. Not something she would have thought he'd do.

God, this man could turn her to mush without even trying.

After dinner, they returned to the boat in the dusky evening. She wanted to sit on the deck and watch it get dark. One of the things she liked best about being away from the city was seeing the night sky with all its stars arrive without the distraction of huge amounts of artificial light. Marius brought out a bottle of wine and they sat in companionable silence. But before she could have more than a couple sips of what he poured for her, she started yawning.

"Tired?" he asked.

"Apparently I am. Guess I'm not used to all that physical work." She handed him her glass of wine. "I better go below and get some sleep if I'm going to be any use to you tomorrow."

"I think I'll stay up on deck for awhile," he said. He stood, leaned toward her, and gave her a gentle goodnight kiss. "Get a good night's sleep. I'll see you in the morning. I'm sorry if I worked you too hard."

"No apology. It was the best day I've had in years. Thank you for it." She went up on her tiptoes and kissed his cheek before heading below.

•••

He drained the last of the wine from his glass then knocked back the rest of hers. Unfortunately, the buzz from the wine didn't muffle the sounds of her rustling around, getting ready for bed. Nor did it stop his mind from asking questions he shouldn't be thinking about. Was she naked between the sheets? She'd slept nude at his house but then, she didn't have anything with her to wear to bed. Did she brush out her hair so it was smooth and tangle-free? The thought of her in bed, those blue eyes lit with desire, her hair spread around her like silken honey, made him hard, well, harder. He'd walked around trying to hide an erection most of the day.

When he'd invited her to join him on this trip, he'd had visions of spending every day exploring the San Juan Islands with her and every night exploring each other in the master cabin. The day part was working out just fine but the rest not so much. At least it didn't look that way right now.

If things didn't change, it was going to take a hell of a lot of wine to get him through this week. Maybe wine wasn't strong enough. Maybe he'd better hunt down something stronger the next time they hit town. Bourbon. Rum. Heavy-duty drugs. Of course, he didn't do drugs and, since he had to stay sober enough to sail the damn boat, excessive drinking wasn't a good idea, either. He sighed. Better resign himself to enjoying the days and gritting it out through the nights. Alone.

He went below, ready to toss and turn in the bed in the main cabin. But as he headed for the sink to get rid of the two wine glasses, he thought he heard her say something. Or was he imagining she had called him because he wanted her to? He stopped listening to the noises in his frustrated brain and concentrated instead on what he thought he heard from the master cabin. Which was nothing.

He took a chance. "Did you call me, Cynthia?"

"Yes, I have a problem. Can you come in and help me?"

"Hold on. Let me get rid of these glasses." He dumped them in the sink then returned to the master cabin door. Slowly he opened it, hoping he'd find what he wanted.

But she wasn't lying naked, her hair spread out around her. She was kneeling in the middle of the bed, her back to the door, shaking her head so her braid moved from side to side. He deliberately didn't look at anything other than the moving braid.

"My hair band is so tangled in my hair I can't get it out. It must have been all that wind today. Would you see if you could get it out, please?"

He picked up the braid, careful not to touch any part of her body, knowing if he did, he might not be able to stop. The elastic holding the braid together was, indeed, badly tangled in her hair. It took him a few minutes to get it all unwound without pulling out too much of her hair but he finally did.

"There. It's out." He tossed the band onto the bed beside her.

She shook her head and the braid began to slowly come undone, slipping in waves across her back. She reached over with one hand, pulled some of the hair across her shoulder then turned to face him. "Thank you," she said, looking up at him with uncertainty in her eyes.

Only then did it register that she wasn't wearing anything but her panties. Her long hair covered one breast leaving the other one bare. The pale pink nipple drew his eyes—and almost his hand.

But he couldn't move. All he could do was stand and stare. Finally, in a hoarse voice, he said, "Holy Mother of God, Cynthia."

Crossing her arms over her breasts, a panicked look on her face, she scooted back on the bed, away from him. "Oh, no, this is so embarrassing. I'm sorry. I'm so sorry."

She was waiting for him to do what he'd wanted to do all day, and he couldn't seem to move. He hadn't had that much to drink had he? Jesus, if he didn't do something in the next few seconds she looked like she might cry. Kneeling on the bed, he put out his hand to her. "No, don't back away. There's nothing to be sorry about. I was just surprised."

She inched a bit closer, near enough that he could reach her to brush the hair off her breast and away from her face. He could see the tension in the set of her shoulders.

"You looked so scared this morning when you first saw the cabin. I didn't want to make you more uncomfortable. I didn't know what you wanted." He shook his head. "Oh, hell, why am I wasting time. Come here." He brought her the rest of the way to him and kissed her, tenderly at first but with more intensity as he felt her begin to relax against him. He took her lower lip between his teeth and nibbled as his hands skimmed down her bare sides. "I've wanted you back in my bed since the afternoon you walked out of my house. But I didn't want you to think that was the price you had to pay for being on the boat. You had to want to be here with me."

He tried to slide off the bed, eager to get his clothes off, to join her but she held on to him as if she never wanted to let go. And she started talking. Babbling, really.

"I didn't know what to do, whether I was supposed to ask you or wait for you to ask me or what. I hoped this was the right thing.

I couldn't imagine ten days of sleeping in here alone. Not when I wanted to touch you, to hold you. Not after the night at your house. And today, with the sunscreen and all this chemistry, this whatever-it-is between us, I was so confused. I wasn't sure. But I thought I'd try…"

He put his fingers across her lips. "Right now I'm less interested in your decision-making process than I am in knowing if sometime in the next two minutes we'll be naked in bed together."

"Yes, but…"

He groaned. "But what, *querida*?"

"But do you have protection?"

His groan turned into a grin. "I'll be back in a minute." He got to the main cabin in about two strides and, when he couldn't find what he wanted by rummaging around, he dumped the contents of his Dopp kit onto the bed where he wouldn't be sleeping that night. He grabbed a box, pulled a foil-wrapped packet out of it and returned to her, both the box and the packet in his hand.

This time, she was waiting in bed as he'd imagined her, hair spread out on the pillow, sapphire eyes in the darkening night now bright with desire, clad only in panties cut high enough to show off her legs and low enough to show her navel, but plain white cotton, which said more than anything about exactly who she was.

He put the box in the drawer next to the bed and the condom on the pillow next to her. "I came prepared."

• • •

It had taken all the courage she could dig out of herself to make the first move. She'd never been the aggressor before. Josh had hated that. And the few other lovers she'd had weren't serious enough for her to try out anything other than responding to their moves. So, when Marius had looked stunned at seeing her barely dressed, she'd been horrified, sure she'd done something wrong.

But now as she watched him shuck his polo shirt, cut-offs, boxers, and deck shoes with a speed that matched what he could achieve in his car, she knew she hadn't.

Moving to the center of the bed she made room for him to join her. "Dear God, you're beautiful," he said as he touched her. "Your breasts…" He never finished the sentence, groaning as he took a nipple in his mouth, twirling his tongue around it, sucking gently, bringing it to a hard point. "I could spend the rest of my life just kissing your breasts," he said. "But I have other things I want to do, too."

She could feel the hard length of him against her thigh, wanted more than anything to feel it inside her, knew she was already wet and waiting for him to enter her. But as long as she was being courageous tonight, she was going to be all in.

"Let me tonight." She pushed at his shoulder urging him to fall back onto the bed. "It's my turn to find out what you like," she said, stripping off her panties then straddling him. Keeping her breasts just out of reach of his mouth, she leaned over him, resting on the palms of her hands, her hair falling onto his chest, tickling, teasing.

He was strong enough to flip her over any time he wanted, she knew, but she was sure he wouldn't. He looked as if he was enjoying her success at surprising him, both in the invitation and the sudden change of position. And she was certainly enjoying it, rubbing her sex against his penis, the contact between his rock hard member and her clitoris just what she wanted, what she needed.

But he wasn't about to give up total control to her apparently. With a sinful grin he touched her, moved against her, bringing her along with the pressure of his cock and with his fingers until she could feel the climax coming, sweeping over her, like a storm of water over the side of the boat.

When she came down from the edge, she whispered, "Not fair. It was supposed to be your turn." Still grinding her hips against him, she dipped her head to pull at his nipples with her lips, then kissed and nibbled at his jaw. Worked up to his earlobe, the curl of his ear, kissing, nipping, then licking softly as if to soothe what her teeth might have done.

"Cynthia," he ground out. "Jesus, woman, you're driving me crazy."

"I want to. I want you to want me more than you've ever wanted anyone."

She leaned over him, her hair and her breasts taunting, teasing him, as she reached for the condom. Ripping open the packet, she sheathed him then straddled him again, intending to lower herself onto him slowly, inch by inch.

But just as she touched his penis, he sat up and she was astride his lap, her breasts crushed against his chest and he'd inserted himself into her so quickly and so deep she couldn't feel anything but him inside her. He straightened her legs and she curled them around his back. In a voice husky with desire he said, "I've never wanted anyone the way I want you. All I thought about all day was being here, just the two of us, having you all to myself, loving you like this. It's all I've wanted." He captured her mouth with his and plundered it, exploring every inch, taking every molecule of oxygen from her lungs. He moved inside her with such urgency that she knew they would both soon climax. She felt his cock grow harder and bigger as they moved in unison toward the inevitable.

"I need you with me, *mi amour.* Come with me now."

Calling his name, she did.

Just before they drifted off to sleep entwined in each other's arms, he whispered, "How long did it take you to get your hair band tangled in your braid like that?"

She laughed. "Longer than I expected. I've been so good at *not* tangling it all these years that I had to work at doing it wrong."

"Any longer and I might have been too drunk to respond."

"Seriously?"

"Pretty close. You might want to keep that mind, if you ever want to try that approach again."

"Will I need to?"

"No, *querida*, you won't."

Chapter 8

"So, captain, where're we going today?" Cynthia asked as she gathered up the remains of their breakfast the next morning.

"Change of plans," Marius said. "Instead of sailing this morning and coming back here for the afternoon, I thought we'd spend the whole day exploring Orcas. You can show me the artist studios and galleries you like. How's that sound?"

Although she'd enjoyed the sailing the day before, a day of looking at art made her heart sing. "It sounds perfect. And relaxing."

"You've looked relaxed since we left Anacortes. I've been envying you. It takes me a long time to unwind when I go away. By the time I've finally gotten there, it always seems it's time to go home."

"You need more down time. You should get out on the water more. If I had a boat like this, I'd be out every chance I could. Like the shoe guys say, just do it."

"Yes, ma'am. Whatever you say, ma'am." He threw her a mock salute.

"Sorry. Did that sound as bossy as I think it did?"

"Not really. You're right. I should. How about this…I'll promise to do better at getting out on the water if you'll promise to crew for me when I do."

She laughed, didn't answer and cleaned up the breakfast dishes.

...

The first thing they did was rent mopeds so they could get around the island. Then they picked up a map at the local Chamber of

Commerce marked with the locations of the galleries and studios open to the public. Cynthia was happy to see so many familiar places and intrigued by a few new ones. First up was a large, well-established artists' co-op where Cynthia knew a number of the artists. She visited with the woman staffing the gallery when they got there, then gave Marius a *sotto voce* critique of all the jewelry and glass in the place. It seemed to amuse him, especially when she wasn't kind.

In the course of the morning, they got through the list of places they had picked out—a goldsmith's studio, where he'd been more interested in the rings than Cynthia would have guessed—a potter's workshop where she came close to buying a bowl she loved—and a smaller co-op. At every stop, she was impressed with Marius's taste for excellent art. He seemed immediately drawn to the best in the place, whether it was a painting, a ceramic figure or a piece of jewelry.

When they stopped for lunch at a little café, she commented on what she'd observed. "You have an awfully good eye. Is it just innate or have you studied art?"

"The only art training I've ever had was the standard kindergarten finger-painting class. And thank you for the compliment. It means a lot coming from you."

"You have some nice pieces in your house. Are they by anyone I would know?"

"I doubt it. I don't buy work based on an artist's name or on some critic's idea of who will become famous or collectable. I buy what I want to live with."

"What's your favorite medium?"

"Not sure I have one. I like painting done with most everything—oil, acrylic, watercolors. And I like interesting photography, ceramics, glass. Lately I've been looking at jewelry a lot."

She smiled. "Yes, thank you for that."

"What's your favorite?" he asked. "Other than jewelry."

"Definitely art glass in three-dimensional. Probably photography in two-d."

"You must have been disappointed today, then. There was less glass here than I expected."

"Yeah, I'll have to remember to tell Amanda about that. Not that she needs another place to show her work. She can barely keep up with the galleries she's in now."

"There was more at the first place we went to, that big co-op. There was also a ceramic piece I think I'm going to go back and buy. Do you mind back-tracking?"

"I'd be kicked out of the League of Starving Artists if I balked at letting a man spend money on art. What caught your eye?"

"It was a figure of a woman. Looked like she was walking into the wind with her long hair and dress blown back until they almost disappeared. It reminded me of a lovely woman I've recently been sailing with."

She let the compliment slide by. "I remember that piece. I liked it, too. But it must be four feet tall. And it'll weigh a ton. You're not planning to get it back to the boat on a moped, are you?"

"I thought maybe you'd ride along side me, we'd lay her across the two mopeds and get her to the moorage that way." He laughed at her startled look. "No, I'm sure they'll ship it to Seattle for me."

Chapter 9

As always, Cynthia woke up with the first light the next morning. She stretched and yawned, feeling more contented, more satisfied, more rested than she could ever remember feeling. Must have been the good night's sleep. Or all the exercise she got sailing on their first day out and exploring the island yesterday. And the wine at dinner—that might be part of it, too.

Oh, who was she kidding? It was because of the long, lovely, languid sessions of sex—of lovemaking—they'd had over the past two nights.

She looked at the man sleeping beside her. He was amazing. She'd never been in bed with anyone like him before. He didn't just have sex with a woman. And he certainly didn't fuck her. He truly made love. He adored every inch of her body.

Still asleep, he was covered with the sheet. It was tempting to pull it away from him so she could feast her eyes on all that male beauty, but she didn't want to disturb a man who hated to be awakened this early in the morning. Besides, she had two nights full of images to think about if she needed to remember his incredible body, his talented hands, his sensual mouth.

It always seemed to take time to get used to having sex with someone new. It was awkward at the beginning, graceless. At least, for the few men she'd been with that had been the norm. It was like you needed practice so you didn't bump various parts of your body clumsily against the other person in an attempt to fit them together with some "eptness"—if there was such a word.

But not with Marius.

He knew how to put it all together the first time. They'd moved in perfect rhythm, like lovers of long-standing. He knew exactly where to touch, what to caress, to elicit a sigh, a moan, a response from her. He knew when to be tender and when to be assertive, when to let her lead and when he should. Both at his house and here on the boat, he spent time discovering what she liked, putting her pleasure before his own, finding places on her body that made her see stars when he touched them, places she hadn't even known existed.

Not that she had a statistically solid sample on which to base her comparison, but she couldn't imagine anyone could be more intense, more tender, more passionate. He was simply a wonderful, unselfish lover.

Last night, after the first time they'd made love, he'd brought wine back to bed for her. She'd curled up after they emptied their glasses, expecting to go to sleep. But he had other ideas. He'd started gently massaging her shoulders, which led to kissing them, of course. Then he did the same to each vertebra in her spine and every inch of her bottom and the back of her legs. She shivered remembering how surprised she'd been to find the backs of her knees so sensitive to his touch.

When he had her trembling with wanting him again, he turned her over and entered her and, with long, slow strokes in and out, he enticed her, excited her, brought her to the edge of orgasm again and again until finally they climaxed in the most intense sensation she'd ever felt. It was like nothing she'd ever known before, like he'd perfected sex and everyone else was just trying to imitate him.

He sighed in his sleep, interrupting her reverie, turning toward her. His handsome face was covered in dark stubble, stubble she'd felt the night before on the inside of her thighs, on her back and legs, the tender skin of her breasts, on her face. God, she probably looked like she'd been sandpapered every place, but it had felt so good when he did it.

And if she didn't stop thinking like this and get away from him, she was going to jump him to get him to sandpaper her again.

Sliding carefully out of bed so she didn't disturb him, she slipped on her shorts and a T-shirt, pulled her hair back in a low ponytail and went topside. It was a cool and beautiful morning, like many other mornings she remembered in places like this, but with a special glow to the day because of that amazing man asleep below in her bed. His bed. Their bed.

Stop. She couldn't let this take over her thinking. It was only one week. Well, ten days. But no matter the exact number of days—or nights—she knew she had to be prepared to give him up at some point. He said as much himself—they shared this special world, here on the boat, just the two of them. And it was the only world they shared. When they got back to Seattle, it wouldn't be the same. She needed to tell him she understood, so he didn't think …

"*Mi amor,* it's cold and lonely in bed without you. Why do you run away from me as soon as the sun comes up?" He was wearing cut-offs and a smug smile that said he knew she wasn't running very fast or very far.

"Don't you want to sleep in? I thought I'd wait awhile before I started breakfast, since I'm the morning person and you're not."

She was sitting with her side against the boat and he sat behind her, enclosing her with his legs, pulling her back against his chest. "There. That's better. Here's where you belong. And the answer to your question is, no, I don't want to sleep in. Not when waking up means I get to do this." He moved her ponytail over her shoulder, tightened his arms around her waist and nibbled on the nape of her neck. "I love the way you taste. You smell like peaches and I keep expecting you to taste like that but you don't. You're spicier than that."

She relaxed against him. "Did you sleep well?"

"M-m-m. And you?" He nipped at her ears between words.

"Of course. You're comfortable to sleep with."

"Comfortable? Ouch. You wound me, *querida*. That's what a teddy bear or a blankie is. Is that what I am?" She couldn't see his face but the fake surprise in his voice amused her. And his continued ministrations to the back of her neck and ears excited her.

"No, you're a wonderful lover, but I assume I'm not the first woman to have pointed that out to you."

"It's only because we have amazing chemistry, and you, *mi amor*, are such a responsive partner." He illustrated his point by licking at the spot behind her ear and blowing softly on it.

She stifled a moan. "Marius, don't! There are a dozen boats around. And sound carries over water so easily."

"So it'll be a little challenge for you. You can't make those noises I love to hear. Which will be a disappointment for me, I admit." He licked and kissed down her neck to her shoulder. "Of course, you can still call out my name but you'll have to do it very, very quietly." By now he was whispering and had his hands up under her shirt, massaging her ribs, moving slowly, inch by inch, to her breasts. "I knew it would be good to hear you say my name when you were in my bed."

"Since you share ownership of the boat with someone else, it's really only half your bed, isn't it? I mean, maybe we've been on your partner's side of the bed for the last two nights."

His hands stilled, as if he was thinking about what she said. "Are you saying you'll have to say my name on the other side of the bed to make sure I have what I want?"

"Something like that."

"Then I suggest we go below now. I thought I had that checked off my 'to do' list and I don't like having to uncheck things." He drew his leg up from around her and stood, motioning for her to follow him.

"Marius, wait. There's something I want to say to you."

"Later, *mi amor*. I don't think there's anything that needs to be said right now other than let's go back to bed."

"No, it's important." Her expression must have looked as resolute as she felt because he sat down next to her and took her hand.

"All right. I'm listening."

She couldn't bear the intense look in those bottomless coffee-colored eyes so, instead of looking at his face, she stared at their hands and played with their interlaced fingers as she spoke. "I just want you to know that I don't expect…don't have any expectations about…you know…about this."

"About what, Cynthia?" The tone of his voice had changed from warm teasing to guardedness.

"About this…you and me. I won't make any demands, won't try to entangle you or trap you. I get it."

"I'm glad you get it, but I don't." He tipped up her face and forced her to look at him. "What is it about being together that makes you…?"

"It's not about being together here, Marius. Being together on the boat is wonderful. It's about later…about when this is over." She shook off his hand. "I'm trying to say it's okay that it'll be different when we get back to Seattle."

"Over? Different? What will be different when what is over?" The tone of his voice was getting uncomfortably chilly.

"I know that when we get back to Seattle, we go back to our own worlds and we don't have a lot in common. I don't expect that you'll, you know, have a lot of time to spend with me, doing the things I do. And it's okay."

He'd been staring at her while she talked, the look on his face now set into a hard, impassive expression. "So, you're saying, what, that you think I won't want to see you when we get back to Seattle? That I pick up women, drag them out to sea, fuck them, then dump them when I'm finished having fun? Is that who you think I am?"

She'd never heard that tone in his voice before. "I didn't mean anything like that. I just wanted you to know that I understand…"

"You understand nothing about me if you believe I'd do something like that." He dropped her hand and rose, his back to her. "I don't know what I've done to deserve your contempt but if that's what you think about me…"

"Contempt? No, Marius, wait. I must be saying this all wrong if you think that's what I mean. I'm trying to say…"

He turned at the top of the steps. "What exactly are you trying to say? Spit it out. Because what I hear is you think I've gotten what I want from you and will drop you as soon as we get home."

"What I mean is, out here, we have our own world. It's like you said, we're together, just the two of us. It's the most wonderful world I've ever been in. If I could, I'd stay here forever." She sniffed back the tears that were beginning to form, knowing she didn't have long before they'd fall. Before that happened, she had to make him understand.

Wiping the back of her hands across her eyes, she continued. "Back in Seattle, it's not like that. We have such different lives. Live in such different worlds, I mean. I just want you to know I understand that. I understand it won't be the same…can't be the same."

"Is this that bullshit you talked about in the bar about being in different leagues? Is that what this is about? I don't know who put that crap in your head but whoever it was really did a number on you. Who was it—your mother? Some man?" She must have reacted to his comment because his expression changed, softened a bit. "That's it, isn't it? Some man told you that. Jesus. No wonder…" He came back to where she was sitting and took her in his arms, nestled her head onto his shoulder. "I apologize for getting angry. But don't put me in the same category as someone who hurt you. Not all men think alike. And those of us who don't think like whoever-he-was might resent your assuming we do."

The tears that wouldn't be held back any longer ran down her face. "Somehow I've turned the best two days of my life into the worst morning of my life and I didn't mean to do that at all. I just wanted to…"

"You just want to ward off what you're afraid will happen because you think I'm like him. I don't know who he was; I don't care; it doesn't matter. Whoever he is, I'm not like that. I would never hurt you that way." He turned her face up. "You have to believe me, Cynthia. Please." He gently kissed her forehead. "Please?"

She nestled into his embrace. "Oh, God, I'm so sorry. I didn't mean to offend you. I was trying to be realistic, to make you understand that I know I'm not the kind of woman you…"

"Not the kind of woman I what? Want to be with? Could fall in love with? What?" He stroked her face with his fingers.

It wasn't until they heard, "Oh, for God's sake, kiss and make up so we can all go back to having breakfast," that they realized they'd been playing the scene out before an audience.

Startled, Cynthia bolted out of his arms, but Marius grabbed her hand to keep her from running. He waved his free hand toward the other boats. "That doesn't matter, Cynthia. This does. Do you trust me or not? I need to know, *querida*."

"I trust you." She shook her head. "But I'm afraid."

Marius stood and put his hands on her shoulders. "Then trust me when I say this: I will never hurt you. You have my word." And then he kissed her. Not the passionate kiss of the lover of the night before, but the tender kiss of someone who was as much friend as lover, as much protector as friend.

When she looked into his eyes after they parted, she saw concern; she saw determination; she saw affection. She saw what might be the future. Sighing she dropped her head onto his chest and he held her.

A few moments later, to the sound of applause and a couple of whistles, he led her below where he got to hear her say his name on the other side of the bed.

Chapter 10

Over the next week, Cynthia learned that she and Marius worked well together at more than sailing and sex. As they hiked, biked, and explored small towns; she found their interests and abilities meshing in surprising ways. It was not just his interest in art but her ability to keep up with him on a bike or a trail and enjoy it. Not just their mutual knowledge of the geography of the islands but their shared interest in the history, too. One thing was different: she was far braver than he was about swimming in the chilly waters around the islands and she made sure she pointed it out to him every time she jumped off the side of the boat.

Even in simple things like sharing meal prep when they ate on board, without working at it, they moved as a team in the small space of the boat. She cooked fisherman's stew; he made arroz con pollo and taught her to make Cuban sandwiches. In the evenings when they were in towns where Marius knew restaurants he liked, they ate on shore and Cynthia always loved the places he'd picked out.

At night, they continued other explorations—in bed—where their activities had gone from great to glorious. Cynthia pretended to be surprised that the bedside table always seemed to have a fresh supply of condoms. But, finally, the night of the seventh day of the trip, when it had been rainy so they stayed on board and in bed all day, they ran out. They'd planned to spend the next day in Friday Harbor anyway, so Marius said he'd resupply while they were there.

After wandering around town for a while, visiting with his friend the coffee roaster and picking up his special roast beans, Marius left her browsing in a gallery he didn't particularly like to achieve his goal.

As she made the rounds, inspecting what was on the walls, beginning to understand why he wasn't a fan of the gallery owner's taste, Cynthia was startled to hear a familiar voice in conversation with a woman. She tried to sneak out of the gallery without running into the person who owned the voice, but he saw her.

"Cynthia? I thought I recognized the back of you. Your braid, I mean. How nice to run into you," Josh Franzen said. He kissed her cheek. "You look great. And you must be doing well with your jewelry, if the articles I've seen in the paper are to be believed. You've certainly gotten some good press lately."

"Hello, Josh. Yeah, I'm doing okay. Great, in fact. I've been very pleased with where my work has gone this year."

"Good. I'm happy for you." There was an awkward pause for a few moments. Then he said, "Oh, I guess you haven't met my… ah…you haven't met Trish, have you?" He waved at a woman who was looking through the print bins, the woman he must have been talking to. "Trish, would you come here, please? I want you to meet someone." The woman wandered over, taking her time, looking first at the jewelry case, then at a pottery vessel on a pedestal before making her way to her husband's side.

When she finally reached Josh, he made the introduction. "Trish, this is Cynthia Blaine, the artist I told you about. Cynthia, Trish… Trish Franzen."

Trish held out her hand in a limp handshake, not looking particularly interested in Cynthia or, for that matter, Josh. "Artist? Oh, you mean the woman who makes jewelry. Hello." She dropped Cynthia's hand and grabbed her husband's arm. "Joshua, there's a print over here I want for the entry hall."

She was about to return to the print bin when she looked over Cynthia's shoulder and her face lit up. "For heaven's sake. Look who's here." She waved. "Now here's someone you really have to meet, Joshua."

Cynthia turned to see who it was, which gave Marius a chance to land a kiss on her forehead as he curled his arm around her waist. "Mission accomplished, *querida*," he said holding up a bag. She blushed then noticed the curious expression on her ex-boyfriend's face. She started to make the introduction. "Marius, this is an old…this is someone I…this is Josh Franzen. Josh, this is…"

Trish interrupted, "Marius, is this where you've been hiding yourself? It has been forever since I've seen you." She had her hand on his arm and was looking flirtatiously at him. "I hoped to see you at the fundraising committee meeting for Bumbershoot, but you weren't there. I guess now I know why. You escaped out here to the sticks. Are you living here?"

"Hello, Trish. No, I'm still in Seattle. Sadly, I only get to sail in the San Juans occasionally. Are you vacationing here, too?"

"Lord, no." She dismissed the idea with a snort. "We're only here because Joshua has some boring meeting to attend."

Marius put his hand out to the other man. "I don't think Cynthia had a chance to finish the introduction, Josh. I'm Marius Hernandez."

"Yes…I mean, hello," Josh said, his curious expression now turned to a bewildering one at his wife's effusive greeting for the man who had just kissed Cynthia. "Nice to meet you."

"Are you staying in town, Marius?" Trish asked. "Maybe we could get together for a drink later. You and your friend, of course. Oh, or dinner. I know a great restaurant here."

"No," Cynthia said. "I mean, no, thanks. We have…" She stopped, unable to think of a credible excuse.

Marius looked quickly at his boat mate then back at the other woman. "Sorry, Trish. We're sailing so we're not staying in town."

Her mouth made an exaggerated pout. "Oh, I'm so sorry. I was hoping…"

"In fact," Marius said, "Cynthia was just hanging around waiting for me to do an errand before we headed to our moorage for the night. And I got what I came for so we should get going." He nodded to Josh and said, "Nice to meet you." To Trish he said, "Good to see you again." After protectively enveloping her with his arm, he said to Cynthia, "Ready to go, *querida?*"

"Yes," she said moving to the door before he finished the question. Then realizing she was being too abrupt, said, "Nice to run into you, Josh, Trish. Enjoy the rest of your stay."

She didn't say much on the way back to the boat. They were docked in Friday Harbor for the evening, so she knew that he'd stretched the truth when he told Trish they had to leave to get to their moorage. But she didn't know how to explain her reaction to seeing Josh again, what to say about him, how to thank Marius for rescuing her from an uncomfortable situation.

When they got to the boat, he immediately poured them each a glass of wine. She started topside but he stopped her.

"Let's have this conversation here, Cynthia." He sat on one of the couches in the main cabin.

She sat opposite him, her eyes downcast. "You want to know who he is, don't you?"

"I know who he is—he's the son-of-a-bitch who hurt you. No, what I want to know is: do you still love him?"

She looked up with a start. "Do I what…? Dear God, no."

"But you did, didn't you? Was he in love with you?"

"He said he was but then he…he left."

"You acted like it was difficult to see him."

"It's just that…just that I haven't seen him in a long time. Really, not since he…since we broke up. It was a surprise."

"And that's all? This is important to me, Cynthia. Are you sure you aren't still in love with him?"

She moved over next to him, linked her arm through his. "Marius, I've just had the best week of my life with you. Two years of being with Josh couldn't measure up to one day with you. Not one day. And that doesn't even take into consideration the nights. I don't know now if I ever was really in love with him. But I do know I don't love him now. And, yes, I'm sure."

There was a long pause before he asked the next question. "Then why was it so difficult to see him?"

She started to protest but he interrupted.

"Don't say it wasn't. It was all over your face how hard it was seeing him…seeing them."

This man saw into her so easily it frightened her. She wanted to deny what he was saying, but she couldn't lie to him. "It reminded me of why he left. Of how I…how he made me feel when he dumped me to marry her."

"Jesus. He actually told you he was leaving to marry someone else?"

"Not exactly, but he didn't have to. He'd made it clear that I wasn't the kind of woman to 'wear the diamonds,' as he put it. I create jewelry with glass; he was looking for someone to wear the real stuff."

"What's he do that he needs a wife who wears diamonds?"

"He and a couple former Microsoft colleagues have a very successful business writing video games and apps for smartphones and tablets. But that's just a stepping-stone to what he really wants. He has political ambitions, wants to be governor. I don't fit the mold of the First Lady of the state of Washington, apparently."

"And Trish does? Is that what he thinks…what you think?"

"Her father is a U.S. senator; her grandfather was in the state legislature. She's connected to enough money in the Puget Sound to finance the campaign it'll take to win the governorship. I've always heard she's, like, Washington political royalty."

"The only thing royal about her is she's a royal pain in the ass. And everyone in her social circle knows it. She's made more enemies than Al Qaeda."

"How do you know that?"

"I've had the misfortune of working with her on a couple committees. She's self-absorbed, tone-deaf when it comes to what anyone else wants or needs, and completely out of touch with normal people. Anyone who's worked with her would refuse to do it again, I think. If he plans to ride to the governor's office on her coat-tails, he may well be disappointed."

Cynthia tried hard not to smile, but couldn't help herself. "His worst nightmare. A high-maintenance woman."

"If that's his nightmare, he's living in hell. I almost feel sorry for him. But, on the other hand, if he hadn't been so stupid, you wouldn't be here with me." He reached for her hand. "You looked so frightened, so unhappy. I wondered if you were over him."

"Believe me, I'm over him," she said with great confidence.

"But you're not over how he made you feel when he left, are you?"

She felt her eyes widen in surprise. "Why do you say that?"

"Because I don't think you are. And that's why you believe I'm going to behave the same way he did."

She started to protest that he was wrong. That she was completely and irrevocably over Josh Franzen. But this man had been able to see into her heart and mind since the first day she'd met him.

"Maybe there's still some of that feeling left. But I'm trying to get rid of it." She smiled at him. "How did you get so smart about me so fast, Marius?"

"It doesn't take an advanced degree in psychology, *querida*. You're easier to read than a billboard about this."

She realized she was chewing on her thumbnail and stopped. "It's just that seeing him, bringing up all that old stuff, made me think again about whether…"

He interrupted her. "I said I'd never hurt you like that and I meant it." He put out his hand to her. "If you want, I can give you character references—old girlfriends, business acquaintances, my mother—who could tell you I always keep my word." His most beguiling smile moved across his face.

Her response was a nervous giggle. "I don't think you need to do that." She moved closer to him and put her arms around his neck. "I'm sorry. I didn't mean for this—for him—to wreck our last few days together." After she pressed a gentle kiss on his mouth, she said, "In truth, just seeing the two of you in the same place made me realize how different you are. I know you'd never do anything like that."

"If that's the case, remind me to thank him the next time we run into him."

• • •

Like every vacation, this one had to end eventually. Cynthia was subdued for most of Sunday as they returned to Anacortes and unloaded the boat. In addition to what was left of the food she'd brought and a suitcase full of dirty clothes, she was taking home a small bowl Marius had bought her on San Juan Island which was even more beautiful than the one in the gallery on Orcas, an ache in her heart that their trip was over, and a sinking feeling that she'd fallen in love with her sailing companion.

As they stowed the remains of their week into the Porsche, Marius seemed to catch her mood. "I'm not ready for this to be over, *querida,* are you?"

"No, I'm not, but it is. We always knew we'd have to get back to reality sooner or later. And later has now turned into sooner… into now." She wiped at her eyes, not wanting him to see how full of tears they were.

He must have seen anyway. He pulled her into his arms and kissed the top of her head. "No tears. It doesn't have to be completely over. Why don't you stay with me until I leave for Central America? It's not the same as being on the boat but at least we'll be together for the next five days."

She looked up at him; sure he could see how surprised she was. "I don't know. I should probably go home. Do my laundry. Get back to my studio."

"Two things: first, I have a washer and dryer at my house. Second, it takes ten minutes to get from my house to your studio." He threw the last duffel bag into the car. "I was wrong. There's a third thing. If you don't come stay with me, I'll be pounding on your door every evening until you let me in and I don't travel as lightly as you do. You'll end up with all my clothes at your house and that'll be very inconvenient for me." His face made clear that inconvenience wasn't the point. He wanted her with him at his place.

"Are you sure? I mean, don't you have a lot to do before you go? Won't I be in the way?"

"You'll never be in my way, *mi amor*, and, no, I don't have a lot to do. The travel arrangements were all made before we left; I got a text yesterday from my assistant that my itinerary has been re-confirmed. All I need to do is pack, which I could do in my sleep, if I had to."

"Okay, then. Okay." She shook her head. "I must be crazy to do this."

"Why? Don't you want to be with me?"

"More than anything. But spending more time with you will just make it harder for me to see you leave."

"Ah-ha. You have uncovered my plan. I want you to miss me while I'm gone so you'll be longing for me to return." His smile was positively lascivious. "That will make you very interested in showing me just how happy you are to see me when I get home."

"Like that wasn't going to happen anyway," she muttered, more to herself than to him, as she slid into the passenger seat of the car.

Chapter 11

If she thought their time in the San Juans had gone by quickly, the five days after they returned raced by in some sort of supersonic blur. Cynthia spent her days at the studio catching up with messages that had come in while she was gone and making arrangements to restock galleries with new work. Marius, to hear him describe it, spent his days on the phone—either with his father and uncles in Miami, their clients up and down the West Coast or his business contacts in Central America.

In the evenings, depending on the weather, they ate the dinners Cynthia prepared for them either at the breakfast bar or on the deck. She realized after the second night that she was cooking all the things she did well, even spending one day making coq au vin, trying to impress him, she was sure. It was funny and pathetic, all at the same time. But she kept doing it. After all, because of him, she was living in one of the most beautiful houses she'd ever seen after spending ten days on his equally beautiful sailboat.

On the evening before he was to leave, however, Marius insisted she join him at the restaurant where they'd had their first date.

Hoping to make it easier on herself emotionally, she moved most of the clothes and things she'd accumulated at his home back to her apartment that afternoon. She thought it would be better to get dressed at her own place for their dinner out. But it didn't work. There was a huge pit in her stomach every time she thought about his leaving that didn't seem to improve by being back in her apartment.

Dressing in what she'd worn to the ballet auction helped a little. She knew he liked the dress. Putting her hair up in a twist made her feel good, too, because she could look forward to having him take it down later. When she was finished—she didn't think she would ever be *ready* to have what she was trying hard not to think of as their last dinner together—she drove to the restaurant.

This time, there was no waiting in the bar. John, the maitre'd, immediately seated her at Marius's table and returned five minutes later with a bottle of Malbec, two glasses and a message. Marius was held up on a conference call and would be about fifteen minutes late.

He was only ten minutes late but apologetic.

"I am so sorry, *mi amor*. Last minute marching orders from above. My father and uncles act like I've never done this before. I get detailed instructions about what I'm supposed to do before every trip, in spite of the fact I've been doing this job for ten years."

"Not to worry. John took good care of me." She poured him a glass of wine.

He took a big swallow before saying, "This was one of those days when I wanted to be the kind of person who drank at work." His expression belied his words, but she knew what he said was, as her mother often described it, "half in fun and all in earnest."

"I've wondered what it would be like to work for family. Does this sort of thing happen often?" she asked.

"No, most of the time it's great. There are times, however, when it feels like I'm in that other kind of family—the organized crime kind—and there's no way out. Today was unfortunately one of those rare days. I don't know if it's different from any place else; I can't make a comparison. I've never worked in any other job. It was planned from the time I left for college that I'd be in the business."

"I don't think I know where you went to school."

"The University of Pennsylvania. Wharton. I did both undergrad and graduate work there. So did my brother."

"Even after two generations of running the business, they wanted you to go to business school? And get MBAs?"

"Especially after two generations of running the business. My father and uncles decided it was time to get some new ideas."

"That sounds amazingly open-minded."

"Don't be too impressed. When we arrived back in Miami with our brand new degrees, my brother Carlos and I, along with our cousin Alejandro, who went to Stanford, were full of all sorts of ideas on how to make the company better. Ninety-nine percent of them were shot down by our father and uncles. The one they actually listened to led, after a few years of research and negotiations, to my opening the Seattle office. I was not happy to discover that my sister-in-law and my cousin's wife had more clout than I did in influencing who would move here."

"Ah, so you lost the coin toss."

"More like the argument. But lately, I have come to be extremely grateful I did."

He took her hand and kissed the palm of it. As he did, the errant strap on her dress slid off her shoulder.

"Damn this thing," she said as she grabbed for it. "I think I'll just cut them off. They're not good for anything except decoration and distraction."

He interrupted her attempt to return the strap to its rightful place. "Leave them. They've been kind to me." Sliding his forefinger up her arm, he caught the strap and slowly, very slowly, inched it upward. "This little piece of nothing allowed me to touch you for the first time. To find out how soft you feel. I'll always be grateful." He leaned in and kissed her shoulder, making her shiver, as she was sure he knew she would.

The maitre'd materialized by the table. "Your dinner will be here shortly. Is there anything else I can do for you, Mr. Hernandez?"

Marius turned away from her but kept his hand on her arm. "No, thank you, John. You did an excellent job of taking care of Ms. Blaine. I appreciate it."

"It was my pleasure. She's an easy person to take care of." He smiled at Cynthia and left as noiselessly as he had arrived.

"Our dinner will be here shortly? You took it way too seriously the last time when I let you order for us."

"I thought it would be nice to have the same dinner we had on our first date."

"Completing the circle, are we? Ending as we started?"

"You make it sound like something is over, *mi amor*. Unless you mean this is the end of the beginning, we're not ending anything. We have a long way to go together."

"You don't have to say things like that, Marius. It's okay. While you're away, you'll have a lot of time to sort things out. Everything has happened so fast with us. You should probably be grateful you have this break."

"I don't need a break and I won't think about anything except getting home to be with you. Why would you think otherwise?"

Before she could answer the unanswerable question, their salad appeared. It was followed by their entrees and eventually a cheese plate. Between bites, they talked about more neutral subjects—her plans to go to Bellingham to see her parents and to take a few day trips to galleries on the coast with new work, some highlights of his travel schedule. She hoped they'd left the previous conversation for good. Thinking about what he might reconsider during his six weeks away was not conducive to enjoying her meal.

It would have been nice to have a romantic moonlit ride back to his house in the Porsche, but they'd driven separately to the restaurant. Besides, when they walked out after dinner, the moon was behind a band of clouds that threatened rain. By the time she got to his house, Marius had already started coffee and had put on some of the Latin music he loved, this time sultry tangos. When she got to the kitchen, after using the key he'd given her to unlock the front door, she put it on the counter and slid it toward him.

"What's that for?" he asked.

"It's your house key."

"I know that, *querida*. I don't know why you're returning it."

"I won't be here anymore."

The expression on his face was puzzled. "Keep it. You might need to get back in the house while I'm gone; maybe you'll leave something. And you'll want it after I get back anyway, won't you?"

Reluctantly, she slipped the key into the small purse she was carrying. He must have noticed her hesitancy because he came around the counter and pulled her to him, kissing her gently on the temple. "Why do I think you're convinced we're having our last night together?"

"No, I don't really think that. It's just that…" She hesitated, burrowing her face into his chest so he couldn't see the fear she was sure was evident in her expression.

"Just that your ex-boyfriend messed with your head and I'm paying—we're paying—the price for it."

She looked up at him with what must have been a surprised expression, if his raised eyebrow was any indication. "Do you really think that's all it is?"

"Yes." He kissed her again, this time not so softly. But he broke from the kiss abruptly and pulled back, his hands on her shoulders, an excited expression on his face. "I have an idea. Come with me. Come see Central America with me." Before she could respond, he said, "I know, you can't be gone for six weeks. You said at dinner you have a lot of work to catch up with. So, join me someplace in a couple weeks. I can show you some beautiful places. Wait until you see the amazing art."

"It sounds fabulous, but one: I don't have that kind of money. Two: I don't have a passport."

"The money isn't a problem but the passport is, obviously." He seemed to be thinking over other options. "All right then," he finally said, "if you can't come with me, live here while I'm gone. That might convince you I mean to come back to you. I'd have to sell the house and everything I own not to see you again." He was smiling a particularly winsome smile.

"Now you're being silly. I'm not going to move in here for six weeks. I'll be fine in my own apartment."

"Please?"

She shook her head. Emphatically.

"The offer will be here as long as I'm gone. Just let me know if you change your mind, so I can warn my neighbor not to call the cops." He went to the living room and pulled something from his briefcase. "I have my itinerary for you. Put this on your refrigerator and circle the last date. It's when I'll be back home, back with you. Until then: text, email. I can't hear from you too often. I'll do the same. But it will be irregular. Some of the places I'm going are remote, no cell reception."

He looked at the paper as if seeing it for the first time. "You know there's another thing we could do—I end up in San Francisco for three days. Why don't you come there to meet me? You don't need a passport to go to California. And I can get you a ticket with my frequent flyer miles."

"You're sweet, but I think we should just let it go for now. Who knows…?"

"I'm not going to change my mind about us while I'm away, Cynthia. Get that idea out of your head." He looked frustrated at the direction the conversation was taking. "But if I can't even talk you into joining me in San Francisco, I guess I'm officially out of ideas on how to convince you I mean it."

She turned so he couldn't see her sad eyes. "Coffee's ready, I think," she said with a catch in her voice. "Shall I pour?"

He didn't respond for a few moments, looking like he was lost in thought. She wasn't sure if he was thinking of another wild suggestion like traveling to Central America with him or if he was reconsidering…no, she wasn't going to go there.

When he came back to her, he said, "I will. Then let's take it downstairs." He poured two mugs of coffee then started for the steps downstairs to his bedroom, motioning her to follow.

The first time she'd seen his bedroom, she'd been struck by the colors. Tonight, all she could do was wonder if she'd ever be there again.

"Let's drink our coffee outside," he said as he pushed a button and the floor-to-ceiling drapes along one side of the room opened to reveal yet another glass wall with a deck on the other side of it.

"I had no idea that was there," she said.

For the first time since they'd gotten to the house, he smiled. "You must have had your mind on other things when you've been in my bedroom."

"Oh, come on, I've been here in daylight," she protested. "Those drapes have never been open. I thought they were just a decorative thing. Instead, they hide the deck."

"I don't open them often. This window faces east and I…"

"Don't like morning. Right." Desperate to get the conversation on a lighter note, she said, "But that might explain why I've been sleeping late since we got back. I thought I was just tired out from crewing on the boat."

He flipped the lights off in the bedroom. For a few moments, it was not only dark but quiet. Then, when he spoke, it was as if he knew she wanted to have a different conversation. He gave it to her. "*Querida!* You mean it wasn't wanting to stay cuddled next to me that has kept you in my bed in the mornings? I woke up every morning this week with you wrapped around me. I liked it. Now you're telling me it was just because the curtains were closed?"

"Well," she said as she stepped out on the deck, "I have to admit that being in bed with you might have had something to do with it."

"Here, join me," he said as he sat on an oversized redwood lounge. When she sat beside him, he put his arm around her and settled her against his chest.

She could hear soft Latin music in the background. "You can hear the music down here, too?"

"In every room. A system it took me a month to figure out came with the house. It was yet another thing I didn't know about until I moved in."

With no light from behind or on the deck itself and a moon still struggling to overcome the clouds drifting past, they were in complete darkness. They sat quietly, sipping coffee for a while as if they were each trying to come up with what would be a comfortable topic of conversation.

After kissing her on the temple, Marius broke the silence. "Not to bring up a difficult subject again but is there anything I can bring back to you from my trip?"

"Bring back to me? You mean, like a present?"

He kissed her again. "Yes, *querida,* I mean like a present."

"You don't have to bring me anything. You'll be too busy working to worry about something like that."

"But I want to."

"Just pictures, then, of all the places you're going. Where I've never been. I'd like pictures."

"And maybe a surprise? Do you like surprises?"

"Not big ones. But I guess I like little ones okay." She didn't want to think what kind of surprise he might have for her when he returned.

He put his mug on the deck and took hers, placing it beside his discarded one. Taking her face in his hand he said, "But no surprises tonight. Tonight I want to hold you and kiss you and love you."

"Oh, yes," she said on a quick intake of breath. "I want that, too." She sat up and faced him. "But first…" She put one leg over his and ran her hands up his thighs.

"There's always a *but* with you, isn't…" He stopped as she settled herself between his legs. "Cynthia, what…?"

She was acting on an impulse. Although her heart was trying to hold on to the idea that he'd come back to her, her brain kept telling her that this might be the last night she'd spend with him. She wanted to make the night special, as good as it could be. A night she—if not he—would always remember. And this was as good a time to do what she was about to do as there had ever been.

"Sh-h-h," she said as she slowly lowered the zipper on his trousers. "Just sit back and enjoy this." She released his stiffening cock from where it was beginning to tent up his boxers, curled her fingers around it and began to massage the shaft, feeling it grow harder and thicker. Even in the dark, she could see his face change from curiosity to desire, swore his dark eyes become darker; heard his sharp intake of breath. When he groaned and whispered her name, it gave her the courage to do something she'd never done before, never wanted to do before to any man.

Slowly, she lowered her head until the head of his penis was between her lips. Running her tongue over the glans, she could taste his salty essence. She licked up one side and down the other, lingered on the tip. As she took him into her mouth, she could feel his member twitch, heard him groan again; felt him buck his hips up towards her. She circled him with her tongue, sucked him further into her mouth, feeling her nipples harden, her breasts get heavy and her panties wet, getting as much pleasure as she was giving.

She didn't know why she had never done this before with him. It was empowering, hearing how he responded to every lick, every touch. She could get lost in just doing this all night, she thought as she sucked and licked.

But he gritted out through clenched teeth, "Cynthia, if you don't stop now, I won't…" He pushed her head away so her mouth came off his penis with a soft "pop."

She looked up at him, her hand still around his shaft, trying to gauge the expression on his face in the dark. "Marius, I want to."

"*Mi amor,* can we continue this in bed, while I can still walk there? While we still have a chance to be in this together?"

"Or, we could make love out here…I mean, if you don't want me to continue with this." Her voice shook as she made the most outrageous suggestion she could ever remember making.

He pulled her up beside him. "So, you're my little exhibitionist. I never knew." Apparently willing to join her in her game, he tugged on the zipper, working her dress down to her waist. When he'd gotten it as far as he could alone, she helped him get it the rest of the way off. In just her heels and panties now, she began pulling at his shirt buttons. He didn't make it an easy task, caressing her breasts and trying to get his mouth all over her while she was unbuttoning him.

Finally, she succeeded and he stripped off the shirt. She had already gotten his trousers open, now she tugged at them, he lifted his hips and she yanked them down. The trousers, briefs, and his shoes ended up in a heap on the deck.

She got on her knees on the lounge chair, put her thumbs under the waistband of her panties and slowly, very slowly began to inch them down her hips. Her reward was a throaty growl and an attempt to hurry her along, but she swatted away his hands and continued with her lazy disrobing.

His patience must have snapped. He took her by the hips and settled her next to him, then finished the job she was apparently doing too slowly. "Off. Now, *mi amor.* We have to get those off."

Her phony protest was buried in his kiss that quickly spiraled out of control, more like a brand on her mouth than a kiss. She slid her hands up his chest and over his shoulders, around his neck so she could pull him closer. Threading her fingers through his hair, she threw back her head and brought his mouth to her breasts. His tongue curled over her nipple, sending shocks from her chest down her torso to where everything was aching with arousal.

He cupped her butt with one hand and drew her closer. His erection was pressing hard against her sex. She'd never wanted anyone more than she wanted him right now. She slid over his body and straddled him, took his penis in her hand and began to guide it into her waiting, wanting body.

He gripped her wrist and stopped her. "Wait, we have to have…"

"Protection." She slid off him, dropped her head on his chest. "We have to have protection."

"It's inside. In the bedside table."

They made an interesting sight walking into the bedroom, she was sure. She was in heels. Period. He was in socks. Ditto.

He must have noticed it too. "You know we are dangerously close to being a porno film, don't you, *querida*?" he said. She must have looked confused because he went on. "Your heels and my socks. And what we were doing outside where we might be caught at any moment. All we need is a pizza delivery boy."

"They all figure in porn flicks?"

"So I'm told."

"So you're told. Right." She made a soft, almost snorty sound.

But one step further into the room and she stopped. In a voice much lower and throatier, she said, "On second thought," she pulled the pins out of her hair and shook it out so it tumbled down her back, "maybe that's not such a bad idea. Maybe I'd like being a porn star…for you." She raised her arms over her head and began to deliberately rotate her hips in time to the sultry music that was playing. When she saw the desire spark in his eyes, she slid her hands down her sides, then up under her breasts. "Come closer, lover," she said in the same husky voice. "Watch me dance for you."

He took two steps toward her, grabbed her around her waist and said, "I'd rather dance *with* you than watch, *mi amor*," and slowly, tantalizingly, moved her, one sensual dance move at a time, around the room and then toward his bed. The feeling of his naked body, his now steely erection against her belly, her soft breasts pressed against his hard chest, the hair tickling her nipples, made her even wetter than she had been. She put her head back and he dipped her so she almost touched the floor, holding her there as he kissed and licked his way from between her breasts to the hollow at the base of her neck.

Why, she thought, did she trust him not to drop her when they were dancing when she had such a hard time believing he cared enough about her to return to her after his trip? Was physical trust so much easier than emotional trust?

"Mother of God," he said as he brought her upright, "I've never been with anyone like you. I'm in lo…" He stopped; his face in shadow and unreadable. He shook his head then sat her down on the bed. Kneeling, he unbuckled her sandals and then helped her pull the comforter down.

After he shed his socks and joined her in bed, he said, "If this isn't what you want, we can go back outside. I didn't mean to interfere with your plans."

"No, it's fine. Here's fine. Anyplace is fine. Just love me." She hurried to talk over the last sentence. "Just *make* love to me." She turned and pulled him to her, her hands all over him, trying to make him forget what she had said.

Chapter 12

Marius had never seen this side of her, this naughty, slightly dirty side of her. Hell, he was willing to bet no one had ever seen it and if he had his way, no one else ever would. Every move aroused him, every kiss was returned with a passion that ate at his soul. When he moved down her body to take her breast in his mouth, she moaned with pleasure at the first touch, gasped at his teeth gently raking over the nipple, shivered when he sucked on first one breast then the other.

And when his hand made a foray down her belly, to the forest of damp curls between her legs, she moved restlessly, pushed at his hand, begging him to touch her where she wanted to be touched; needed to be touched. As he complied, his fingers in her hot, wet core, she came undone in his arms.

So exhausted was she by her orgasm that she fell asleep almost immediately. He watched her for a while, stroking her hair, listening to her soft, sleeping sounds then he carefully left the bed. When he'd gathered up their clothes from the deck, he came back to the room and closed the drapes. She was awake, looking around the room, as if confused.

"Hello there. I was afraid I'd lost you for the night," he said.

"Where were you? I thought…"

He held up the armload of clothes he was carrying. "It looks like rain. I wanted to bring all this in."

"Oh, yeah. Good." She put her arms out to him. "But we weren't finished, were we?"

He dropped the clothes on a chair, pulled a condom from the bedside table and slid in beside her. "I'll never be finished wanting to make love to you, *mi amor*, you know that."

"Show me." She grabbed the condom and pulled him toward her.

It was his intention to go slow, to make love to every inch of her body before coming inside her, but when he saw those sapphire eyes that seemed to be reflecting light from some mysterious source look up to him, he knew he didn't have a chance of taking it slow. He kissed her, took the breath from her lungs and sucked her tongue into his mouth. Filling his hands with her breasts, he felt the hard tips of her aroused nipples, smelled the scent of her, the mix of peach and arousal he wanted to bottle and take with him.

Tearing open the condom wrapper with her teeth, she covered him, barely getting it on him before he had to roll over her, part her legs with his and enter her. She wrapped her arms and legs around him, her nails dug into his back as he drove deep into her, knowing he would never want another woman after Cynthia. Never love another woman after Cynthia. He was lost in her. Completely lost.

• • •

Three hours later, he was still awake, although she had drifted off to sleep after a second round of lovemaking. It had never been just sex with Cynthia, even though that's what he had thought it would be at the start. He knew now it had always been making love.

He fought sleep, not wanting to waste the last few hours of being with her. He could sleep on the plane. Where he wouldn't be holding her. Wouldn't be able to touch her silky hair, listen to her soft breathing.

How he was going to get through six weeks without her, he didn't know. Somewhere in the past few weeks, his fun summer with a beautiful blonde had turned into something else. He didn't know when or how. But he'd fallen in love, deeply in love, with her. She was everything he never thought he'd find in one woman—sexy and beautiful, yes, but more importantly, warm, loving, talented, and smart. She made him laugh; she made him *want* at a level he never knew himself capable of. She made him want to abandon his plans for a well-ordered life in Miami for whatever life with her would be like. He could no longer imagine living anywhere unless it was with her.

And he was afraid of telling her because he didn't know if she would believe him. If she would just hear the same words Josh had said before he left. If he could get his hands on that SOB, he'd make him pay for not only wrecking his own relationship with Cynthia, but what Marius wanted to have with her, too.

Punching out Josh Franzen had a certain appeal right now. It would channel the frustration he felt about failing at the other things he'd been trying. Tonight, for example. He'd set it up to remind her of how magical that first evening together had been. Instead, it seemed to have made her feel like he was saying good-bye for more than just six weeks. Nothing had worked out right, not the place, not the meal, not even going along with her impulsive idea to have sex on the deck.

So now what? What the hell did he have to do to convince her this was real, he was real? All he could think to do was to live up to his word. Come back to her so she would see he meant it. Then tell her he loved her and wanted them to make plans for a future together. Maybe that would do it. He hoped so. It was about all he had left.

In her sleep, she nestled against him, her soft curves fitting perfectly against his body, her peachy scent enveloping him. In spite of the two times they'd already made love, he wanted her again. Hell, he couldn't think of any time in the past month he hadn't wanted her.

It was going to be a long, long six weeks.

• • •

The next morning was difficult. Trying to keep a cheerful expression on her face wasn't easy. She kept trying to smile, only to find her mouth resisting the effort.

He teased her, "I'm not going off to war, *mi amor*. It's just a business trip."

"I know," she put her arms around him and snuggled her head to his shoulder. "It's just been so perfect lately. I'm not looking forward to being without you, that's all. I'm going to miss you like crazy."

"Then my work here is done. That's what I was aiming for." He kissed her temple before disentangling himself from her embrace. "And none too soon. I have to get to the airport. Want to drive my car or yours?" He pulled his keys out of his pants pocket and dangled them in front of her.

"You'd really let me drive yours?"

"Of course."

"I'm not sure this is the best time for me to drive it. I may be a little distracted."

He dropped the key ring onto the counter. "All right then. If you'd rather, we'll save that experiment until I get back. Unless you want to give it a try while I'm gone. I'll leave the keys here. Maybe you'll want to take it on one of your trips to the coast."

She drove her car to the airport and went in with him, standing at the security gate, watching him walk down the concourse until she couldn't see him any longer, wondering—fearing—this was how it would all end; having him fade off into the distance until he was like some mirage of water in a desert.

Chapter 13

Six Weeks Later

Had Portland always been so far away from Seattle? It had never seemed to take this long to get there before. Or was it these damned cars and trucks headed south, slowing down the traffic? Cynthia drove miles over the speed limit when she could, driving like Marius in the Porsche—no, she couldn't think about that, think about him. Not until she had a chance to talk with Amanda. Why the hell was it taking so long to get there?

Like a good best friend, Amanda hadn't questioned Cynthia when she'd called and said she needed to come to Portland—right now. Amanda had just answered "of course" when Cynthia asked to stay with her because she needed to be away from Seattle.

So here she was. Back on I-5 trying not to think about Marius Hernandez, closing yet another circle. Only this time, the tape in her head was longer and full of things she wasn't sure she wanted to think about.

Funny, the time he'd been gone on his business trip was longer than the time they'd spent together. But they'd been in constant communication with each other and it seemed like they'd actually grown closer over the weeks. He courted and seduced her in long emails, lots of texts—in fact, they'd texted so many times, she'd come up against the limits of her data plan for the first time. And there were phone calls, during which she could hear him say he missed her and was counting the days until he came home, instead of just reading the words.

He described the places he was visiting, places she'd only read about or seen in movies: Costa Rica, Guatemala, Honduras, Panama, Nicaragua, Mexico. From places he said he would take her some day, he sent her the pictures she'd asked for via his iPhone—coffee plantations, exotic flowers, picturesque villages, big cities, even some of him with his coffee growers. Those were the ones she looked at every day. Her handsome Marius. Well, handsome Marius. She was still not sure he was really hers. Although she was more sure than ever that she was his.

She'd done everything she could to keep busy. She'd taken new work to Bellingham and visited for a couple days with her parents, gone to galleries in Tacoma and Olympia and on the Long Beach peninsula, shipped new work to Liz in Portland.

Gradually, the weeks passed, the end was in sight. She was counting the days until he got home, eagerly looking forward to seeing him. Until just a few days ago.

She pulled up in front of Amanda's house in Northeast Portland, took a deep breath and went to the front door. Time to face it.

Amanda and Chihuly, her curly-coated retriever, greeted her and led her to the kitchen where her husband, Sam Richardson, was working on his laptop. As always, Sam had a kiss for Cynthia. Then the three of them settled in around the kitchen table to visit until Sam got bored with glass and art gossip and left for his daily run, creating the opportune moment for Cynthia to tell her friend why she was there.

But Kat, Amanda's six-month old baby, woke from her nap and needed attention, a clean diaper, and some food. Cynthia didn't mind. She was Kat's godmother and hadn't seen her in awhile so she fussed over the baby, eliciting the kitten-like purrs that had been the genesis of her nickname.

By the time that was all taken care of, it was close to five. Amanda pulled out a bottle of wine, set a glass in front of Cynthia and suggested they go into the living room to talk.

"I'll pour you a glass of this and we can get comfortable and chat. I'm still not drinking because I'm nursing, but you shouldn't have to suffer because of that." She uncorked the bottle and was about to pour when Cynthia pushed the glass away.

"No, no thanks. No wine for me either."

"You don't have to join me in my non-drinking."

"I know. I'm just not drinking right now."

Amanda laughed as she opened the refrigerator to return the bottle of wine. "I never thought I'd hear you say that until you got pregnant." Her hand froze on the refrigerator door. Then she whirled around, the bottle still in her hand. "Oh, my God, is that why you're here? You're not pregnant…are you?" She inspected her friend's face. "You are, aren't you?"

Cynthia gulped hard before saying out loud, for the first time, "Yeah, I'm pregnant."

Amanda waited, seeming to expect her friend to say something else, but when Cynthia merely played with the empty wine glass, she said, "I can't tell from your face if you think this is good or bad."

"I haven't decided how I feel about it. I just took the pregnancy test—well, a whole bunch of pregnancy tests—yesterday. And I'm still stunned."

"It's none of my business, but didn't you…?"

"Yes, we used protection. Every single time. But sometimes, even the most careful precautions don't work."

"I know. I'm sorry. I didn't mean to sound judgmental."

"You didn't. I'm just a little defensive. And sensitive. On top of being stunned."

Amanda put the wine and the glass away before asking the next question. "Have you told Marius? What did he say?"

"I haven't told him. He's still out of town; he won't be back in Seattle for another few days. And this isn't something I wanted to tell him in a text message. Or even on the phone. I want to see his face when I tell him, so I can see how he really feels." Cynthia played with her braid for a few moments.

She continued, "That's why I'm here. I'm avoiding him. He's in San Francisco and I'm sure he's been trying to call me, but I've been ignoring the phones, not looking to see who's called. I don't know what to say, how to talk to him, without sounding weird. I even left home without my cell so I wouldn't be tempted to answer it."

"How were things when he left?"

"Good. They were good. After our vacation in the San Juans, I stayed with him for five days until he left on this trip. It was so comfortable; it was almost like we'd lived together for years. I got a little antsy about his leaving, wondering if he was coming back, but I've heard from him regularly since he's been gone, just like he said."

"Do you love him?"

"God, yes. More than anything in the world."

"Does he love you?"

"He hasn't exactly said it. He said he cares for me, calls me *mi amor*, my love. He signs all his messages with love and always says he misses me. He acts like he does, but he's never said the words. I don't know. I'm…confused, I guess, would be the best description."

"Okay, let's leave him out of it for now. Suppose he's not in the picture. What would you do then? Would you terminate the pregnancy?"

"That was my first impulse. But the more I thought about it, the less it seemed like what I wanted to do. It doesn't feel like the right choice for me. I'm almost thirty years old. I've always wanted to have children. This may be my only chance. If he walks away, I think I can do this on my own." She looked up at her friend and asked plaintively, "Can't I? I mean, do you think I can?"

"Sweetie, you can do anything you set your mind to. Since we were in college, I've watched you do things I wouldn't have been brave enough to try. I had a trust fund to fall back on when I decided to follow my heart and be an artist. You didn't and you've made it work. But don't you think you should give him a chance first, before you decide you'll have to do this on your own?"

"I guess."

"He deserves to know. But whatever you decide, I'll be there for you—we'll be there for you—every step of the way."

Just as Amanda pulled her friend into a hug, Sam walked back in. He looked at the two women. "This looks seriously not about glass. What'd I miss?"

"Girl stuff," Amanda said. "But I think it will require you to be a single father this evening."

"I've done that before," he said with a grin. "My boys will tell you I do okay with it."

"Except that Sammy and Jack are much happier with the meals they get on their weekends with you now that we're married and you're not making them eat green eggs and ham for dinner."

"True. But at this stage of her life, Kat's not in any danger of having to put up with my abysmal cooking. I can manage to get a bottle of breast milk into her without incident. And I'm hell on dirty diapers." He started for the steps before asking, "Why am I going to be alone with my daughter tonight? Not that it matters. Just curious."

"I'm dumping you as my date for the opening of the big glass exhibit at the Art Museum and taking Cynthia instead. I'll call and cancel the babysitter. You don't mind, do you?"

"Christ, no. I forgot we were supposed to go to that. It's not that I don't enjoy looking at glass, but I had a helluva week. A quiet evening with my daughter is much more appealing than the thought of standing around the Art Museum making small talk. In fact, to show you how much I appreciate being able to stay home, I'll volunteer to get take-out for us after I have a shower. Can't go to one of those things on an empty stomach."

• • •

Cynthia hadn't brought anything even vaguely appropriate for an opening night at the Art Museum and Amanda was much shorter than she was, so there was no chance of borrowing clothes. Amanda insisted that a new dress and a pair of frivolous shoes would make her feel better. They waited for Sam to finish his shower then took off for the nearest Nordstrom's.

On the way there Amanda giggled like a kid, reliving all the times she had taken over dressing Cynthia for a big event or an important date when they were in college. While Cynthia had never been much interested in clothes and make-up, Amanda had been a pro. This was her chance to see if she'd lost her touch, she said. She didn't want to get out of practice before Kat grew up and needed her.

It was obvious she was still as good as she'd been in college. When they arrived at what she deemed was the appropriate department, she corralled a saleswoman, told her what they—well, she—was looking for and joined the woman in tearing through racks of clothes on a mission to find just the right dress. So serious was the search that observers must have thought she was dressing Cynthia for tea with royalty.

Ten dresses made their way back to the dressing room where Cynthia was required to strip and try them on. As far as she was concerned, all of them were great, but Amanda was more critical: this one was too dowdy, that one too trashy, most were too ordinary or not enough something or another. Cynthia wasn't always sure. Finally, the clear winner emerged.

The dress Amanda liked best—and Cynthia agreed was beautiful—was a soft peach color that complimented Cynthia's fair skin and tawny hair. Its halter-top accented her breasts; the snug bodice showed off her trim waist; the short skirt bared enough of her long legs to make shorter women—read: Amanda—jealous.

To complete the long-legged look, the saleswoman brought a stack of stiletto heels from the shoe department for her. After trying them all on, Cynthia picked a pair of peep-toe, sling-back pumps with four-inch heels the exact color of the dress. She rationalized she'd be able to wear the shoes with other dresses, even though she knew she owned nothing else that color. She signed the required credit card slip without even looking at the total. In the grand scheme of her life at the moment, hundreds of dollars in unnecessary clothing was nothing. After a quick stop at the cosmetics counter for the right foundation and lipstick, they were on their way home.

Once back at the St. Claire/Richardson house, Amanda went to work on Cynthia's hair and make-up. The up-do she created was more elaborate than anything Cynthia could have done by herself. Her make-up was professional yet subtle, again, more than anything she would ever contemplate much less accomplish on her own.

By the time they were finished, they were laughing, talking about some of their adventures in college, stories that Amanda swore Cynthia to secrecy about. There were things, she said, that were part of their college experience she had no plans to share with her daughter until Kat had at least a master's degree and three children of her own.

To accessorize the new dress, they raided Amanda's jewelry collection. Over the years, she had purchased enough of her friend's work to have a nice selection from which to choose. They agreed on an early necklace that featured elaborate coral orange and pale green beads and had matching earrings.

Amanda dressed while Sam fetched dinner from their favorite Thai restaurant. All through the meal, Cynthia was nervous about dribbling Pad Thai on herself but she survived without a spill. At seven-thirty, after Amanda had fed Kat one more time and pumped enough milk to tide her over for the rest of the evening, the two women left for the opening.

Chapter 14

The Portland Art Museum sits on the South Park Blocks, a twelve-block linear stretch of tree-lined quiet in the heart of the city. The two women were early enough and the evening pleasant enough that Cynthia asked to walk through the park before they went inside. It had been a while since she'd spent time there and this had been one of her favorite places when she was in college, after the Reed campus itself.

She loved not only the old trees that shaded the park but the public art on each block: Teddy Roosevelt on his horse looking his Rough Rider best. A modern installation of granite pillars called "Peace Chant." A fountain donated by a Polish immigrant early in the twentieth century in gratitude for the success he'd found in the city.

Old churches flanked the green space as well as the Art Museum, Portland State University, the Historical Society, and the Performing Arts complex. For Cynthia, it was the real heart of the city, the place where she found a sense of peace and purpose.

By the time they finally went into the museum, she was calm and happy, eager to see the old friends Amanda assured her would be there. The "old friends" included not only artists and collectors they knew but also familiar glass art pieces. On display were some works they'd seen before, some they'd read about in books, and some they recognized by knowing the style of the artists who'd created them.

Loaned by a number of Portland studio art glass collectors, the pieces in the exhibit demonstrated the amazing range of modern glass art. The centerpiece of the exhibit was an installation by Dale Chihuly—a chandelier of spring green glass hung above a glass garden of bright reds and darker greens. The display was bracketed by a number of his seaforms, Persians, and baskets.

But that was just the beginning. Two pieces by Amanda's mentor, Jessica Loughlin, were there. So was an elegant pitcher and goblet set by Dante Marioni. Next to them were Silvia Levenson's iconic pink glass hand grenade and barbed-wire-decorated high heels. Pieces by Klaus Moje, Narcissus Quaqliata, William Morris, Catharine Newell, and others were there, too, including—Amanda had failed to mention beforehand—two pieces of her work.

For Cynthia and Amanda, it was like being turned loose in a candy store. They weren't sure where to go first. For at least an hour and a half, they went through the exhibit, seeing pieces they knew well, discovering a few they'd never seen in person, discussing their favorites and how those artists had influenced their own work. Cynthia felt relaxed for the first time in thirty-six hours, grateful her friend had suggested she socialize. The evening out was just what she needed.

As they were beginning a second round of the exhibit, Liz Fairchild and Collins joined them. Amanda's work on display had been sold through Liz's gallery and she was thrilled to see the pieces there, as well as the husband and wife who had purchased them. Collins, who was thinking about incorporating glass in a large sculptural piece he was creating, got Amanda excited about the idea. They had decided to continue the discussion over dessert someplace when Liz glanced across the room and spluttered, "God damn. Son of a bitch."

"What's going on?" Amanda asked, looking to see what had prompted Liz to swear.

Liz pushed her partner toward the other room. "Nothing. I think I missed some of the exhibit next door, that's all. Let's go back there and leave that way."

"No, we saw everything in there," Cynthia said, turning towards where Liz was looking. "This door is closer to…" Seeing what Liz was trying to keep from her ended her sentence.

Marius was there. With a woman.

At first, Cynthia thought she was imagining him because it reminded her of her fantasy of his social life. He was standing across the room, looking like he owned the place, holding a glass of champagne. Unlike her fantasy, though, he wasn't in a tux; he was in one of his dark business suits.

But the other piece of her fantasy was there—a beautiful brunette holding a glass in one hand and Marius with the other, her voluptuous body as close to his as she could get it. She wasn't dressed in the ball gown Cynthia had imagined his date would wear; rather she was in a black mini-dress with a very low neckline and not much on her shoulders. Her black heels were even higher than Cynthia's new ones.

She was also wearing a Cleopatra collar with clear and opalescent white beads.

Until that moment, Cynthia had never understood what people meant when they said they'd felt their stomachs drop. But watching him with another woman, realizing this was no fantasy but her worst nightmare, she felt it. Most of her insides took a nosedive, seeming to drag her balance with them. She felt dizzy, like there was no blood in her brain, sure she must be ghost-pale under her make-up. The irrelevant thought that she was grateful Amanda had insisted she wear make-up flitted across her mind before it was squashed by the thought that Marius was there with another woman.

Liz grabbed her arm. "Let's get the hell out of Dodge before he sees us."

But it was too late. Before they could leave, Marius saw them. For a few seconds he looked like he didn't believe his eyes; seemed to react as Cynthia had originally, as if what he was seeing wasn't real. Then his expression changed. He looked puzzled. Or maybe he was just stunned that he'd been caught. A smile began but didn't take hold of much of his face.

Cynthia didn't know if she was more angry or humiliated. He'd lied. About where he would be. About her—about that woman. And if he'd lied about those two things, he'd lied about everything. That was what made her angry. But how humiliating that he thought it would be okay to show up at an exhibit he must have known her friends would attend, flaunting his friend, his *girlfriend.*

The woman with him was talking, seeming not to realize he wasn't paying attention. Then she appeared to ask him a question. When he didn't respond, she looked in the direction he was staring and saw four people glaring back at her.

"That son of a bitch," Liz repeated. "I thought he was a gentleman, that he was…"

Amanda waved off the rest of the sentence, put her arm around Cynthia and said, "Come on, Cyn, let's leave. He doesn't deserve the time of day from any of us. We'll just walk out."

"No," Cynthia said. "I'm fine." She pulled herself up to her full height, stuck out her chin and tried to look like she believed she really was okay. "I won't let him make me run away."

"I doubt that you're fine, but we'll do whatever you want," Amanda said. "Maybe *he'll* have the sense to leave."

Instead, he walked toward them.

"Oh, shit, he's coming over here," Liz said. She took a position on the other side of Cynthia, leaving Collins to stand alone, looking puzzled at what appeared to be a wall of women facing the man coming towards them, trailed by the woman in the black dress trying to keep up with his long strides.

Marius stopped in front of Cynthia, took her hand and tried to draw her to him. "*Querida,* I couldn't believe my eyes. You didn't tell me you would be here. Is that why you haven't been answering…?"

She shook off his hand and stepped back. "Yes, I'm here. How was your trip to Central America?"

The puzzled look was back. "You know how it was. I told you."

"Oh, well, you also told me you were going to San Francisco, yet here you are in Portland, so I wasn't sure I actually knew how your trip was either. Assuming you actually took the trip." Before he had a chance to respond, she said, "Collins, this is Marius Hernandez. Marius, this is Collins. You know the rest of the group."

The woman in the black dress and the Cleopatra collar had caught up with Marius and had linked her arm through his. Cynthia looked at her. "I'm sorry," she said, "I don't know your name or I'd introduce you, too. I'm Cynthia Blaine."

Marius said, "This is Isabella Rodriguez, Cynthia. Bella, Cynthia is the artist who created your collar." He untangled his arm from hers. But Bella was determined. When she returned her hand to the crook of his elbow, he didn't try to remove it a second time. He had the grace to look uncomfortable about it, however.

Cynthia didn't know brown eyes could be cold, but Bella's were. At least, when she looked at Cynthia they were. "Oh, yes, didn't I read something about you in the Seattle paper awhile ago? Nice to meet you. You must be enjoying seeing the work of such well-known artists. I imagine it inspires you to get better."

Amanda's arm tightened around Cynthia. Her friend's voice was as cold as Bella's eyes when she said, "Cynthia Blaine is one of the best at what she does. It seems she wasted a piece of her better work on someone who doesn't appreciate it."

Marius looked both uncomfortable and angry. "Don't be rude, Bella. Cynthia's work is much sought after. I told you that when I gave you my family's gift."

"Sorry. Didn't mean to offend," Bella said in a tone that was anything but repentant.

Marius continued. "These are friends of Cynthia's." One at a time, he indicated the other three people. "This is Amanda St. Claire—I pointed out two of her pieces a few minutes ago.

Collins—I'm sure you've seen his work in the sculpture garden in Seattle. And Liz Fairchild."

"Are you an artist, too, Lynn?" she said to Liz.

"It's Liz, and I own a gallery where spoiled women like you come in and complain about the price of work they don't understand." She turned to Collins. "I think it's time we all left, don't you?"

Collins, who looked like he was still trying to figure out what exactly was going on, quickly agreed. Amanda kept her arm around Cynthia as they walked away without saying anything more.

They'd almost made their escape when Cynthia felt a hand on her shoulder and smelled a familiar spicy scent.

"Wait, Cynthia. You can't just walk out like this."

"Yes, I can," she said. "It's exactly what I'm doing." It made her sadly pleased to see the pleading look in his eyes.

"Let's go someplace where we can talk without distractions. Please."

"I think you've said all that needs to be said this evening without uttering a word. And your 'distraction' is waiting for you." She waved towards Bella Rodriguez who was standing in the middle of the room glaring, her arms crossed over her chest. She looked like she would start tapping her foot at any moment.

Amanda looked back and forth between her friend and the man who was holding on to her, as if trying to decide whether to hit Marius or drag Cynthia away. Finally, Cynthia nodded to her that she could leave. Amanda walked away, out of earshot, to where Liz and Collins were waiting. And watching.

Cynthia turned back to Marius and shook off his hand. She was happy to see he looked worried, as well he should be. He'd been caught. She could see a muscle in his jaw working and frown lines around his mouth and in his forehead.

"You're reacting to something you got all wrong." He put out his hand, tried to touch her again but she stepped back, out of his reach.

"I don't think so. I think I've finally got it absolutely right. Go back to your date. I need to leave with my ride." She gestured toward where Amanda was waiting for her.

"She's not my date. You're not being fair," he said, anger now tingeing his voice, too. "I called to tell you…"

"Tell me what, Marius? Another lie? Tell me you're in San Francisco on business when you were here in Portland on a date? Oh, wait. You already told me that lie. Tell me that the woman you gave the Cleopatra collar to is 'just a friend'? No, you've already told me that one, too. That you…" She stopped, hearing how her voice was rising in volume with every sentence, seeing people turn around to look. Not only was she on the verge of creating an uncomfortable scene but she knew if she kept talking she'd cry. And he was not going to get the satisfaction of seeing he could make her cry.

She had to get out of there.

But just as she was about to leave, Bella joined them. "Marius, it's time for the ceremony. I have to go over there. Please. I don't want to do this alone." She put her hand on his arm. He looked pained, glancing back and forth between the two women.

"I'll be there in a minute, Bella, as soon as I finish this conversation. You go ahead and I'll join you."

"I'm counting on you. You promised." Bella left, glancing over her shoulder several times as she made her way to the microphone now set up in front of the Chihuly centerpiece.

"Cynthia…" His voice sounded defeated, exhausted.

"Go, your date needs you. And she doesn't strike me as the type who has much patience with waiting." Without letting him say anything more, she walked rapidly to where Amanda, Liz, and Collins were waiting. Amanda put her arm around her as soon as she reached them.

"Are you okay?" her friend asked.

"No. I need to get out of here. Now."

She kept from crying until they got to Amanda's house. But as soon as she got into bed, she started and couldn't stop. Amanda must have heard her because after what seemed like an hour, but was probably only ten minutes, her friend appeared with chamomile tea.

In silence, she drank the tea and Amanda rubbed her back. The tears subsided eventually.

"I feel so helpless. Is there anything I can do?" Amanda asked, pulling her friend's head onto her shoulder.

"Can you get Sam to arrest him and put him in jail for a long time?" Cynthia asked. She knew Amanda's police detective husband would do just about anything for his wife. "If he had to live without his expensive car and his custom tailored suits for a year or five it might make me feel better."

"If he could, he would. You know Sam loves you." Amanda removed the hair band from Cynthia's braid and began to unravel it. "What are you going to do about telling him? Marius, I mean. About the baby."

"Nothing. I'm not going to do anything. I may never tell him. He made up my mind for me tonight. I'll do this on my own. It's clear from what I saw that I can't trust him. Not with my feelings and certainly not with a baby." She sat up and put her arms around her friend. "Thank you for taking me there tonight."

"Really? If I hadn't made you go, you wouldn't have seen him."

"I wouldn't have known the truth. And I needed to know it. So, yes, thank you." She yawned.

"Why don't you try and get some sleep. We can talk about this in the morning."

"I don't want to talk about it anymore. In the morning I'm going home and picking up my life where I left off before Marius Hernandez got in the way. But sleep is a good idea. I am suddenly very, very tired."

Chapter 15

For Marius, the evening at the Art Museum had been a disaster on every level. Cynthia's reaction, he supposed, was understandable given that she thought he was in San Francisco. But she wouldn't let him explain why he wasn't. Nor would she explain why she hadn't returned the dozen or so messages and texts he'd left on her phones telling her about the change of plans. He couldn't even get her away from everyone to find out why she was so quick to think the worst. Of course, even if she'd been willing, he doubted that her band of friends would have let her go out in the Park Blocks with him alone, which was what he wanted.

And then there was Bella. She pouted like the spoiled brat she was, behaved badly in front of Cynthia and her friends, and almost made a scene when he didn't immediately follow her for the opening ceremony. This was one of those times when family obligation was the bane of his existence.

As soon as the formalities opening the exhibit were concluded, he'd dragged Bella out of the museum and taken her to her father's house. She'd screamed at him most of the way there about humiliating her in front of all of Portland by chasing after another woman when he was at the event with her. She'd raked him over the coals about being a bad friend when he'd been there to support her in her "hour of need," as she kept insisting it had been. He'd responded that she was behaving like a selfish child and he was sorry he'd ever agreed to go with her.

He didn't even walk her to the door when he got her home, just watched from his rental car to make sure she got inside safely before heading for his hotel. They parted on such bad terms, he was sure Bella would call his father and report his behavior like he was some sort of errant schoolboy.

He was tired from his trip, wrung out by what had gone on at the museum and unsure how to go about making it right with Cynthia. Trying to figure how to get her to listen to him without interference from her friends kept him awake half the night.

The one thing he had figured out was, if the evening at the Art Museum had been bad, the next day held the potential of being even worse.

It lived up to his expectations.

Knowing Cynthia stayed with Amanda St. Claire when she was in Portland, as soon as he got out of bed, after a very short and not very restful night, he started looking for where Amanda lived. He tried 411 and drew a blank. When he searched online, he found her website and an email address, her exhibition schedule, dozens of images of her work and the websites of every gallery where she exhibited but no address or phone number. Not surprising, probably, but frustrating nonetheless. He knew Amanda was married, but didn't know if she shared a last name with her husband, although he assumed she didn't as there were no St. Claires, male or female, listed in Portland.

After he exhausted all the on-line alternatives, he was left with one option—and it wasn't one he looked forward to. The only way he could think to find Amanda's address was to convince Liz Fairchild to give it to him. So he headed for Northwest Portland to The Fairchild Gallery, steeling himself for whatever price Liz might extract for giving him what he wanted. He was willing to take whatever she dished out as long as he ended up with a way to reach Cynthia.

He arrived ten minutes before the gallery was due to open. Through the glass door he could see Liz at the rear of the gallery, talking on the telephone. He didn't knock, knowing she'd eventually come to open the door and he didn't want to interrupt her phone conversation and make her any more angry at him than she already was.

However, it was neither a knock nor the need to open the gallery that drew her attention to him. Whirling around, making what looked like a dramatic point in the conversation, she saw him at the door. She looked shocked, then angry, immediately turned her back to him and let him cool his heels at the door until she was ready to end her conversation and let him in.

To say she was inhospitable was to underestimate her venomous tone by a considerable amount. "What the hell are you doing here? Haven't you caused enough trouble already?" she asked.

"I'm not trying to cause trouble, Liz. I'm trying to repair the damage from last night. Can I come in and talk to you? Please?" He tried to take a step into the gallery but Liz blocked his way.

"What would I want to talk to you about?"

"The obvious. Cynthia."

"I don't think there's a single thing I care to discuss with you in regard to that subject. Although there's a whole hell of a lot you need to talk to her about. If she'll talk to you. Which I doubt."

"Look, I know I need to straighten things out with her, but I don't know how to find her. She's not answering her phone or returning my…"

"After what you put her through at the Art Museum? Do you blame her?"

"She wasn't answering her phone before that. Is she staying with…?"

"And why the hell do you think I'll tell you where she is? You have brass balls, Hernandez, if you think I'm going to help you hurt that poor woman any more than you've already done."

"I don't want to hurt her; I want to talk to her. Hell, I never intended…"

"You never intended what? To humiliate her by flaunting your girlfriend in front of her and her friends? Didn't you think dating other women when you've been practically living with her would hurt her?"

"Bella's a family friend. We weren't on a date. Her father…"

"She was hanging on you like you were a Christmas tree and she was tinsel. That's not how my family friends act."

"I'm not responsible for…"

"Of course not. You're not responsible for being so overwhelmingly attractive that women hang all over you, are you?" Her expression was positively poisonous. "What arrogant male bullshit. I really thought you were better than that."

Marius was silent, even after she'd finished her rant.

"Don't you have anything else to say for yourself?" Liz asked.

"When you decide to let me finish a sentence, I do. And I'd prefer to do it inside unless you want to continue being performance art for the neighborhood."

He saw her look at the passersby walking slowly, pretending to look in her gallery's windows but actually enjoying the conversation they were eavesdropping on. "All right. You can come in. I'll give you one minute to finish enough sentences to convince me I should help you."

He stepped into the gallery and Liz closed the door before pointedly looking at her watch. "One minute. Go."

"My father asked me to come to Portland to attend the funeral of an old and dear family friend—Bella's father. I called Cynthia a dozen times to tell her about the change in plans, but she wasn't picking up so I could only leave messages. After the funeral, Bella stayed in Portland to wind up her father's affairs. One of which was the glass exhibit where some of Mr. Rodriguez's collection was on display. She thought she needed to be there to represent the family, but didn't want to go alone. I agreed to go with her as a favor to a woman who'd just lost her father." He took a deep breath. "Is my time up?"

"Keep going. You've got my attention."

"Bella has always been spoiled and indulged by her father. She's young and scared and right now…"

"She's looking for another man to spoil and indulge her?"

He was surprised at how astute Liz's observation was about a woman she'd seen for only a few minutes. "Possibly. I've never seen her behave that badly before. She knows I'm in love with Cynthia, but that didn't seem to change the way she was acting. Then, after the conversation with all of you, she was embarrassed, accused me of deliberately humiliating her in front of everyone and yelled at me the whole way to her father's house. So, in the course of one fun evening, a family friend who'd just lost her father, the woman I love, and three of her friends all ended up pissed at me."

"Is this the truth, Marius?"

His mouth curved into a half smile. "Thank you. At least I've progressed from Hernandez to Marius. And, yes, it's the truth."

"Why didn't you tell us all this last night?" Liz moved further into the gallery, leading Marius toward her office.

"I tried and got shut down."

"You didn't try hard enough."

"I probably didn't. I was jet-lagged, out with a badly behaving family friend and facing a wall of angry females surrounding Cynthia. It was escalating into a nasty scene and I couldn't deal with it. I thought—I hoped—Cynthia would at least talk to me long enough to let me explain what was going on. I was wrong." He wiped his hand over his face, feeling tired and out of gas.

Liz seemed to see him clearly for the first time. "You look like hell. Like you could use a cup of coffee."

"I could use a gallon of coffee. I didn't sleep much last night."

"In my office, I've got coffee and Amanda's address and phone number. That's where Cynthia stayed last night. I don't imagine she slept any better than you did. Maybe you can catch her before she leaves to go back to Seattle."

...

Half an hour later, he was in the Alameda neighborhood where Amanda lived, having decided he wouldn't risk a phone call, fearing that would only make Cynthia run again, this time for who-knew-where. And he was too tired to go on a wild goose chase. If he was going to have to chase, he wanted to know where he had to go. He would either find her here or find a way to convince Amanda to tell him where Cynthia had gone.

He sat in his car by the curb for a few minutes, finishing up the third cup of coffee Liz had given him and getting up his courage to tackle what was going to be another tough conversation. Finally, he walked up the driveway to the door. The first response to his knock was the bark of a dog; the second was a man with sandy brown hair and a wary look who opened the door. Somehow, Marius was sure the man had been watching him from the house.

"Can I help you?" the man asked. He was holding the collar of a large, black, curly coated dog.

"My name is Marius Hernandez," he began.

The man's expression turned from wary to curious. "You've got guts. I'll give you that. I'm Sam Richardson, Amanda's husband."

Marius asked, "Is Cynthia here?"

"She was. She left early this morning for home."

"Damn. I hoped…"

"Who is it, Sam?" Amanda appeared behind her husband, a baby in her arms. She clutched the baby tighter when her eyes caught sight of Marius. "What the hell are you doing here?"

"That seems to be the universal greeting for me this morning. Liz said the same thing."

"Is that how you found me? You tortured Liz?"

"I explained to Liz that I needed to talk to Cynthia. And once I explained why, she gave me your address, yes."

"Remind me not to speak to her again," Amanda said. "She's a traitor."

"If you'll let me explain…"

"Explain what? That you're a bastard? I don't need to hear an explanation for that. I already know it."

Sam stepped back from the door. "Maybe you should come in and talk to my wife in the living room." He waved Marius in. "And I'll take Kat, pretty lady. You're holding her so tight, she might not be getting enough oxygen." He took the baby from his wife's reluctant arms. "I'll leave you two to figure this out between yourselves. And good luck, Hernandez, you're gonna need it." He headed for the steps with his daughter, calling for the dog to follow him.

Amanda glared at him. "Well, what do you have to say for yourself?"

"Can we sit down?"

"I'm fine standing up and you won't be here long enough to get tired of being on your feet. Say what you have to say and leave."

He gave Amanda the same short version of what he'd been doing in Portland he'd given Liz. When he was finished, she dropped abruptly into the chair she'd said she didn't want to sit on.

"Oh."

"I tried to tell you all at the museum without making too much of a scene, but I couldn't get past your wall. I understood why you were doing it but it didn't make it easy for me to explain what was going on."

"So you've talked to everyone now?"

"I went to see Liz this morning. She was reasonably gracious…"

"That's saying a lot for Liz." He thought she was close to smiling.

"Reasonably gracious after she gave me hell. But she told me Cynthia was staying here, gave me your address and phone number. I'd been trying to call Cynthia for two days but she wasn't picking up."

"She wasn't answering the phone before she left Seattle and she didn't bring her cell with her."

"I wanted to see her, not just talk to her, that's why I hoped she was still here. She didn't say she wasn't."

"Didn't say she wasn't? Then you talked to her?"

"Yeah, isn't that what I just said? I talked to her this morning. She gave me hell but once I explained it all, she was okay. She forgave me. That's how I got here."

"She forgave you. Then you know why she was upset."

"Of course I know why she was upset. I'm the one who upset everyone."

"No, I mean beyond what happened last night. She told you about the baby."

"The baby? What baby?"

Chapter 16

"Cynthia didn't tell you she was pregnant?"

"How could she tell me anything when she won't talk to me?" He wasn't sure if he was more surprised, worried or anxious. "Pregnant? Mother of God. She was all alone when she found out, wasn't she? She must be terrified. That's why she was in Portland. To see you, not go to the glass exhibit."

"Won't talk to you? You said you talked to her. That she forgave you."

"Liz…Liz forgave me. Why would I be here if I'd already talked to Cynthia? I'm here because I hoped she'd be with you." He started toward the door. "I have to get to Seattle."

"This is awful. I had no business telling you. I have to call her, explain."

"NO!" He whirled around and reached for Amanda as she picked up the phone.

Sam walked back into the room just as Marius grabbed Amanda's arm. He took two quick steps toward his wife.

"Let her go, Hernandez. Now." His hands were in fists as he spoke. He put his arm around his wife, pulled her against him, turning sideways to shield her with his body.

Marius may not have recognized Sam's cop face but he heard the ring of authority in the low, hard tone of his voice. He dropped Amanda's arm and put both hands in the air. "Sorry. I didn't mean anything by it."

Amanda patted her husband's arm. "I'm fine, Sam. After what I just did, Marius has every reason to be angry at me but he's not going to hurt me."

Marius dropped his hands but hoped the pleading tone in his voice would be enough to convince Amanda. "Please don't call her. I don't want her running again. Let me talk to her first. I have to make sure she's all right."

Amanda squirmed out of Sam's protective embrace and went to Marius. "I'm so, so sorry. I should never have said anything. Please forgive me?"

"I'm not angry. And there's nothing to forgive. I'm glad I know. I just want to talk to her before she gets it in her head to run again, to Bellingham or Pullman. I'd never be able to convince her parents or her sister to let me talk to her." He closed his eyes for a moment and wiped his hand over his face. "She needs to know she doesn't have to deal with this alone. That it's okay. We'll make this work. Together."

Amanda looked at Marius, her big hazel eyes wide. "Oh, my God, you love her, don't you?"

"Of course I do. I spent most of my free time for the past month trying to think of ways to persuade her to marry me."

"And you're not freaked about her being pregnant?"

"Surprised, yes. Freaked, no. This may be just what I need to convince her I'm right about us being together. About marrying me. I expected an argument from her."

Amanda threw her arms around him and kissed him on the cheek. "Go. Get to Seattle. Tell her what you've told me. And have her call me when she stops crying."

• • •

He finally caught a break or two. No cop was lurking on I-84 as he roared out to the airport at speeds that would have gotten him one hell of a ticket if he'd been caught. It took less time than usual to turn in the rental car and there was a seat available on a plane to Seattle that left a half-hour after he bought the ticket. He even had enough time to get more coffee into his tired body before he boarded the plane.

In flying time, it's only an hour from Portland to Seattle. Before Marius boarded the plane, he was sure it would seem longer than his flight from Panama to Portland, he was that anxious to get home. But once he was on the way, he wondered if an hour was enough time to prepare for the most important conversation of his life, at least his personal life.

If she wouldn't listen to him, if she turned him away, he didn't think he'd ever find with another woman what he'd found with her. He had spent the two years before she'd come into his life assuming he'd eventually return to Miami. Now all he could think about was what kind of life they'd have in Seattle, the two of them.

And their kid. Their kids. Kid. Whatever. He'd come from a big family; he'd always thought that once he found the right woman he'd have a big family, too. But if she wanted this baby to be an only child, he'd happily go along with it. Anything to make her happy. To keep her his.

He took a small box from his jacket pocket. Held it for a moment, then opened it. Inside was a gold ring, the setting a delicate design of swirls and loops with a diamond set in the center and two sapphires flanking it. The design was one he'd traced from memory, based on a piece of her jewelry he'd seen her wear. The sapphires were exactly the color of her eyes.

He'd had it made for her by a goldsmith in Honduras, a family friend. Now, all he had to do was get her to accept it. That was what he'd been struggling with before he got to Portland—coming up with a way to accomplish that. But he had no idea how to get it done. You'd think by now he would stop trying to make plans about anything with this woman. This would have to be purely seat-of-the-pants. He hoped like hell whatever he came up with when he saw her was successful.

"You need to fasten your seatbelt, sir. We're about to land in Seattle," the flight attendant said. She looked at the ring in his hand. "That's beautiful. I've never seen anything like that."

"Thank you. It's for a unique woman so it had to be very special."

"She's lucky. Are congratulations in order?"

"I certainly hope so."

The flight attendant winked at him. "I think she'll say yes. I would."

...

Cynthia had left Portland right after breakfast, if a cup of tea and a piece of toast qualified as breakfast. The smell of coffee had made her slightly nauseated that morning. She blamed the pregnancy but maybe it was something else, like betrayal by a handsome coffee broker. She hoped not. She really liked coffee.

Apparently for this trip on the interstate, there was a bulletin out that she was desperate to be home and all the traffic stayed out of her way. By eleven, she was in her studio, surrounded by familiar sights and sounds—the hiss of the propane torch, the translucent colors of the glass rods, the sight of them bending to her will as she shaped her beads in the flame. She hoped that having to pay close attention to the molten glass and high temperature flame might keep her from thinking about anything else for a while.

It worked. Hours slipped by. She wrapped finished beads in wire, wove silver strands into elaborate designs and soldered metal together for neckpieces and cuff bracelets. On the torch, she warmed up, then melted, glass from long rods onto a coated mandrill, shaping round, oval and square beads.

Once finished, the beads went into her small kilns for a controlled cool-down to prevent them from breaking. Pleased with her new designs, she was intent on beginning to create the beads she wanted to incorporate into the cuff bracelet she'd been working on. She missed the sound of her studio door opening, apparently, because when she heard a very familiar male voice say, "When were you planning to tell me?" she was startled.

Even through the tinted lenses of her protective glasses and the glare of the propane flame, she could see that Marius, who was standing just inside the door of her studio, looked tired and unusually serious. Either that or he was mad as hell at her. Surprised either by his expression or by his being there, her hand jerked and the glass rod she was holding, which hadn't been warmed up yet, hit the flame and shattered into bits when the cold glass came in contact with the heat.

"Damn it," she said, standing up quickly enough that the stool she was sitting on fell over, clattering loudly as it did. However, she wasn't fast enough to get away from the pieces of broken glass that spattered on the front of her shirt, melting into the fabric.

She didn't see him move but suddenly Marius was in front of her, brushing off her shirt, asking, "Are you all right?"

"I'm fine, no thanks to you." She pushed his hand away and took off her glasses. "What the hell are you doing here? Shouldn't you be with your 'friend' or whatever you're calling her now?" She shook her head and turned off the torch before she was tempted to use it on his carefully pressed shirt and trousers. Even tired and terribly serious, he was beautiful to look at. Damn him.

"Oh, good. A perfect three," he said.

"What's that supposed to mean?"

"Three times being greeted the same way in the same day." He picked one more piece of glass off her shirt. "I've been polite enough to answer your question, now it's your turn to answer mine: when were you going to tell me?"

"Tell you what?" She pretended to inspect her shirt for more glass, trying to avoid looking at him. Trying not to smell his aftershave or think about what it felt like to curl up in his arms or how his mouth tasted when she kissed him or …

"That we're having a baby."

She was sure she looked stunned. But she recovered quickly. "*We're* not having a baby. *I'm* having a baby."

"Don't tell me it's not mine. I know you weren't with anyone else while I was away."

"Why, because you're such a world-class lover that no woman wants any other man after she's been with you? Is that what Bella tells you?"

"I know you, Cynthia," he said softly, "It's not in your nature to hook up with someone while you were sending me texts and emails every day. You'd never do anything like that."

She picked up the overturned stool and sat on it. "Whatever. It doesn't make any difference. I'm having this baby by myself. I told you when we were…I told you already. I've never had any expectations about what was…about us. No demands. I'm not trying to trap you or entangle you. So you can breathe easy; you're off the hook."

"My breathing's just fine the way it is, thanks. And suppose I don't want to be off the hook? Suppose I want to be entangled?"

"Who with? Bella? She sure looks like she wants to be entangled with you. I'm surprised she's still not wound around you like a snake." She hated herself for sounding so nasty, so jealous.

"Bella has nothing to do with this…with us."

"There is no 'us.' You made me realize that last night."

"There most certainly is an 'us.'" He moved directly in front of her, put his hands on her shoulders. "There's been an 'us' since the first time you walked into my house. I knew you belonged there and you did, too."

"I did not." *God, could she sound any more childish and unconvincing.* "Even if I…" She shut down the rest of the sentence. He wasn't going to distract her. "It doesn't mean anything now. Not after last night." It had been a mistake to sit down. She had to look up at him, couldn't move to get his hands off her shoulders. Not that she really wanted to shake them off. If this was the last time she saw him, she wanted to remember how it felt to have him touch her, what the warmth of his hands on her skin felt like. She had to stop herself from lowering her head to rub her cheek against his hand.

"It means a great deal to me that there's an 'us.' Because last night I realized what a mistake I'd made. I should have…"

"Not lied to me?"

"Let me finish, *querida*. I realized I should have told you how much I love you before I left. I wanted to. But I didn't know if you'd believe me. So I decided the way to convince you I loved you was to live up to my word and come back to you. Now I know it was a mistake. Not telling you is what made you run."

"No, seeing you dating another woman in Portland when you told me you were in San Francisco on business is what made me run."

He paused for a few breaths. "Have you looked at your phones since you've been home?"

"My phones? No, I came right to the studio. What do my phones have to do with anything?"

"You'll find messages on both your cell and your home phone and a couple of texts telling you I had to go to Portland for a funeral. I asked you to drive my car to Portland so I wouldn't have to wait to see you until I got to Seattle. But I never got a call back."

"Oh." She thought about it for a few seconds. "But if you were there for a funeral, how come…?"

He ran through the explanation about Bella, her father's death and the opening at the art museum.

She was sure she looked as skeptical as she felt. "That sounds just a little too pat. What'd you do, practice it all the way here?"

"I imagine it does sound rehearsed. It's the third time today I've had to give that particular explanation."

"Who else did you practice it on?"

"Liz, who granted me one minute to convince her I deserved to know Amanda's address. Then Amanda, when I went to her house where I thought I'd find you but only found your angry friend."

"Your charm must have been working overtime to get both of them to tell you everything. I thought I was going to see *my* friends when I went to Portland. But I guess they were your friends. Otherwise why would Amanda rat me out to the one person she knew I wasn't going to tell about being pregnant."

"It wasn't like that. She misunderstood what I said. She thought I'd already talked to you and you'd told me about our baby."

He said the words "our baby" so softly, so sweetly. She wanted to believe he cared about it as much as she did. Needed him to want this as much as she did. But she couldn't bring herself to hope. Not yet.

"If Amanda had done something like that, she'd have called me right away to explain."

"I asked her not to. I was afraid you'd run again. She said to call her when you stopped crying."

"Why would I be crying? I'm mad, not sad."

He touched her face where a tear was making its way down her cheek, wiping it away with the pad of his thumb. "Yes, *mi amor*, I know you're mad."

"Don't call me that. I'm not your love. I'm not anything to you. You lied…you weren't…you don't…" When tears choked her and she stopped talking, he pulled her up from the stool and wrapped her in his arms.

He kissed the top of her head. "I didn't lie. And I do love you, *mi amor, mi corazon*. You're my love, my heart. I've spent hours over the past month thinking of ways to convince you to marry me."

"You don't have to marry me because I'm pregnant," she said between shuddery breaths, pulling away from him.

"You're not listening. I was thinking of ways to convince you to marry me before I found out about our baby."

"Our baby…" She closed her eyes to keep more tears from forming. "How did…?"

He drew her back against him and she didn't resist. She felt his smile against her hair. "I remember the 'how' very well, *mi amour*. I thought about it often while I was gone. Every night, in fact. "

"I didn't mean it like that," she said. "You know what I meant."

"It doesn't make any difference now, does it? I'm not sorry. In truth, it's probably the only way you'll say yes to me."

"Say yes? To what?"

"When my sisters were pregnant, they never had difficulty hearing, but you seem to." He took her chin in his hand. "Having to suggest marriage more than once to get an answer seems excessive, but you're worth it. So, I'll repeat myself. For the past month, I've been trying to figure a way to get you to say you'll marry me. Not because we're having a baby, but because I love you, because you love me. Because I've known since the first day we spent together that you're the woman I've been looking for."

She saw what she now realized she'd always seen in his eyes—love, respect, determination, maybe a little amusement. "Marry you?"

"Marry me. You're already mine. You've been mine since the first time we made love. But I want to make sure you stay mine for the rest of my life. For the rest of your life, our lives together. If I can't convince you with my words, maybe this will convince you." He pulled a small box from his jacket pocket and handed it to her.

She looked at it. "What's this?"

"The present I brought you from my trip. I had it made for you by a goldsmith I know in Honduras."

She opened the box. "It's a ring." When she looked up at him, she felt her tear-filled eyes widen. "A beautiful ring."

"Yes, *querida,* an engagement ring. The diamond is traditional. The sapphires are the color of your eyes. The design I remembered from one of your neckpieces. So—and this is time number four or maybe even five—marry me." He took the ring from the box and slipped it on her finger. It fit perfectly.

"Marry you. But…" She stared at the ring, unable to think coherently.

"No more 'buts.' I want you to come home with me now. We'll sort out when we're getting married after we talk to our families. For now, just come home with me."

"Home?"

"Yes, home. We can move your things from your apartment over the next week. We'll combine your things and mine, whatever you want, into our house. We can put what we don't have room for into storage for when we move into a bigger house."

"A bigger house?" She was beginning to wonder if she would ever again have anything to say that didn't echo something he'd just said.

"When our family gets too big, we'll move someplace larger. But always where we can see the water. I promise."

She sniffed back a tear and bit back a smile. "You have this all figured out, don't you?"

"I've been thinking about it for a month."

"I haven't agreed to any of this and already you've planned out my life for me. Suppose I don't want to marry you or live in your house?"

He looked devastated. "You don't love me?"

"Of course I love you. You have no idea how much I love you. I just don't like being told everything's settled before I even have a chance to say anything."

Taking her face in his hands, he gently kissed her forehead, her eyelids and her lips. "You're right. I shouldn't be making all these decisions alone. You have every right to think it over. I'll just wait while you think about it. Let me know when you decide." He went back to her mouth again, took her lips in a fiery kiss that melted her knees and most of her insides. "You don't mind if I keep kissing you while you decide, do you? It'll give me something to do while you think."

She took a step back from him. "You know I can't think when you kiss me."

"No," he said with a half-smile. "I didn't. But it's good to know. I'll keep that in mind. The information might come in handy."

She was playing with the ring on her finger as she watched his face, looking for…for what? He'd said everything she'd ever wanted to hear from him. And what he'd already said was written right there on his handsome face. Had been all along.

Taking a step back toward him, she put her arms around his neck, buried her fingers in his hair and kissed him as thoroughly as he had kissed her.

"Okay. I've thought about it. I'll marry you."

"Thank God. Now let's go home." He took her hand and started to the door.

"Wait. First, I have to close up the studio."

"What can I do to help get us out of here? I want to get some food into the house before I fall asleep."

She handed him a dustpan and broom, pointing out the remains of the broken glass rod. He laughed and started sweeping them up.

"It sounds like you think you've covered just about everything," she said as she began to put away her tools. "But I bet there's one thing you haven't thought about."

"What's that, *mi corazon*?" He dumped the glass shards in the trashcan and put the broom away before coming behind her and nuzzling her neck.

"How in the world are we going to get a car seat in the Porsche?"

About the Author

Thanks for reading *Trusting Again*, book number four in the Second Chances series. I hope you enjoyed getting to know Cynthia and Marius. If you're curious about the other two couples in the story, check out *Beginning Again*, the story of how Liz and Collins met, or *Loving Again*, which tells Sam and Amanda's story. Oh, and there are two more books in the series, one due out in October 2013, the other in early 2014.

If you'd like to keep in touch, here are a few places where you can find me:

My website and blog: *www.peggybirdwrites.com*

On Facebook: *https://www.facebook.com/pages/Peggy-Birds-Authors-Page/ 264392460308782?__req=6*

On Twitter: *https://twitter.com/peggybirdwrites*

On Pinterest: *http://pinterest.com/writingbird/*

One last thing: I always like to know what readers think of my books. So if you'd write a review on Amazon or Goodreads with your honest opinion, I'd appreciate it. Thanks so much.

More from This Author
(From *Together Again*)

Instead of the peace and coffee she'd been looking for before boarding her plane, Margo Keyes's latte came with a side order of idiot-on-a-cell-phone. Anyone within twenty feet of the man in the blue blazer heard some of the conversation. Where she was sitting, it was in Dolby digital surround sound.

It figured her trip would start like this. She'd been apprehensive about it from the get-go. Not that she had a fear of flying. It was the landing—or rather, what was waiting for her *after* she landed—that was the problem.

Her chance for quiet acquisition of caffeine courage diminishing by the second, she glared at the man in the blue blazer, hoping he'd take the hint and shut up. Too intent on his call, he seemed to miss what was, she was quite sure, a stunning look of disapproval.

"Are you interested or not?" he yelled. Allowing no answer to what was apparently a rhetorical question, he continued, "If you don't want what I've got, I know someone who does. So, what's it worth to you?" After he paused, presumably for the response, he said, "Good. I'll let you know what the bid is after I talk to my other customer." He ended the call, shoved his phone in his pocket and glared back at Margo before storming off.

Walking down the concourse, she consoled herself that if the coffee break hadn't worked, at least she had a business class seat reserved on the plane and a hotel suite waiting at her destination. She'd indulged in both, rationalizing if she was making this trip at least it should be comfortable. Interesting concept, that; comfortable discomfort.

As the plane taxied out to the runway, she pulled out her BlackBerry to review her schedule for the next ten days, hoping some magic wand had been waved over it, making it all shiny and fun. However, as usual, her fairy godmother was AWOL. She put her head back against the seat and closed her eyes. What the hell had she been thinking, saying yes to this? Ever since she'd moved to Portland, she'd restricted her Philadelphia visits with her mother to long weekends in the spring and fall. It got her points for being a good daughter, avoided too much time being fussed over and kept her out of the two East Coast seasons she didn't like. This trip? Ten days in mid-June when she'd just been there two months before.

Checking the airline schedule online, she found a flight home the day after the presentation she was to give the following week. That would cut three days off the trip. But before she could change her reservation, the flight attendant asked her to turn her phone off.

Nothing left to do but work. She opened her stuffed-to-the-gunnels messenger bag and took out what she'd brought to help her craft her speech. It looked like she'd included everything in the courthouse except the old law library. Being tapped as the last-minute stand-in for your boss at an important conference will make you do that.

While trying to organize it all, she lost track of her jacket. She eventually saw it too far under her seat to grab and asked the person sitting behind her to get it for her. A man threw it back. When she turned to thank him he added a dirty look—a familiar dirty look. Shit. The man in the blue blazer from the coffee stand.

Finally settled, she began to review case files. Unfortunately, the steady stream of orders to the flight attendants from the seat behind her distracted both her and the cabin crew. When she'd read the same report three times and still didn't know what the hell it was about, she gave up trying, put her work away and replaced it with her iPod. By plugging in the ear buds she could drown out ABB ("Asshole in Blue Blazer," as he had now morphed into being) with Pink Martini, Colbie Caillat, Suzanne Vega and Alicia Keys.

By the time she'd worked through most of her current favorite albums, the pilot announced their imminent arrival in Philadelphia. Winding the cord for the ear buds around the iPod before stashing it away, the thought occurred that ABB had now wrecked a second part of her day. Two strikes against her and she hadn't even gotten to the hard part yet.

The man jumped up as soon as the plane's wheels hit the ground, arguing with the flight attendant when she insisted he get back in his seat. He sprang into action again as soon as they arrived at the gate, rooting around in the compartment above Margo like he was hunting for truffles. Fearful he'd dump out the contents of her messenger bag she stood, too, and removed it from the overhead.

"Out of the way," ABB said. "I'm in a hurry."

"We all are," Margo said. "But they haven't opened the door yet."

"I have to be out of here when they do. Move, bitch."

"Excuse me? What did you…?"

The man grabbed his briefcase and pin-balled his way through passengers and cabin crew to the door, which was still closed. "Asshole in Blue Blazer" moved ahead of "walking across the country pushing heavy beverage carts" on the list of reasons she was glad she hadn't followed up on that girlhood fantasy of being a flight attendant so she could get paid for traveling.

At baggage claim, still thinking of comebacks for ABB, some of which were anatomically impossible, most of which were too obscene to say out loud and many of which were both, she let her bag go past a couple times before she realized it had made an appearance. Off balance when she snagged it, she swung around awkwardly, smacking into someone behind her. When she started to apologize she saw, much to her consternation, she'd whacked—guess who?—talking again on the phone.

Echoing her sentiments, ABB said, "Oh, hell, you again. Just what I need," and elbowed past her. He grabbed the briefcase leaning up against the luggage belt in front of her, and ran toward the taxi stand, leaving her apologizing to empty air. "Welcome to Philadelphia, Margo," she muttered to no one in particular as she pulled out the handle from her suitcase.

At the exit for the rental car shuttles, she hesitated long enough to inhale one last little bit of cool, clean air. Thus prepared, she forced herself out the automatic door into the wall of hot, wet vapor, which, laced with vehicle exhaust and the effluvium of the nearby oil refineries and storage facilities, was what passed for air during summer in her birthplace.

Oh, yeah, welcome to Philly.

• • •

A short, stocky man in a business suit paced on the spongy ground, wiped his forehead with a handkerchief and swatted away a bug. He hated this weather. When he delivered what he was about to get, he'd be on the next plane out of here.

A taxi approached and he stepped back into the shadow of the trees. The car's interior light illuminated a man in a dark blue blazer paying the driver. After the cab peeled off, the stocky man emerged from the shadows and beckoned.

The two men walked silently into the copse of trees. When they were hidden from the road, the stocky man asked for what he'd contracted to purchase. The man in the blue blazer said he had another offer that the buyer had to meet or the deal was off. The stocky man shook his head. The man in the blue blazer pulled out his cell phone and punched in a number. He handed the phone over after the call was answered. The stocky man said a few words in a foreign language before handing the phone back to its owner.

While Blue Blazer was focused on winding up the phone conversation, the stocky man reached under his jacket and pulled out a gun. His problem eliminated, the gunman pulled the blazer-clad body further into the trees and covered it with branches.

Taking the phone and the briefcase, he returned to his car. When he searched the briefcase, he discovered that what he wanted wasn't there. Nor, he found out when he went back and searched the body, was it in the fucking blue blazer. All he had was a flash drive with what he'd already seen and a pissed-off buyer waiting for what he now couldn't deliver.

• • •

In her rental car and headed toward Center City on I-95, Margo went over, again, what she had ahead of her. The shoes she'd packed said it all—Manolo Blahniks for a high school reunion she'd been conned into attending, mid-heel pumps for the conference where she was to give the still-unwritten presentation and the flats she wore to please her mother who hated running shoes. No shoes were needed for the other thing niggling at the back of her mind.

In Portland, where she was a thirty-something deputy district attorney, Margo's colleagues thought it was great she was going for a longer-than-usual visit with her mother. She'd explained her reluctance was because she didn't like the summer weather. But it wasn't just the weather she didn't want to face. There was the world of Daisy Keyes to deal with.

"Daisy" was what her maternal grandmother, for whom she was named, had called her. It was the literal translation of Margherita, her given first name. Margo was grateful no one else had joined her *abuelita* in that folly. What the hell had she been thinking? Daisy? Really?

What made it worse was she thought of herself as a wilted daisy that last year of high school, at the mercy of people and events over which she had no control. Now Margo would be spending an evening with people she largely avoided when she visited her mother, all of whom she was sure remembered only too clearly what had happened that year.

But a suite at the Bellevue would help. No memories there. And, she noticed as she looked around the lobby while waiting to register, no guy in a blue blazer either. She crossed her fingers that she'd seen the last of him. All she had to do was unpack and freshen up and she'd be ready to face whatever was waiting on Fir Street.

• • •

Margo and her mother, Dolores Campbell Keyes, had grown up in the same house in South Philadelphia. The three-story row house with a marble stoop and a deep-set entry had been her mother's dowry when she married Kenny Keyes. Nothing about it had changed since her grandmother had lived there, except the rest of the neighborhood.

After circling the block for only five minutes, Margo found a semi-legal parking spot, made sure nothing valuable was visible and locked up the car. As she approached her mom's house, a man called from the direction of the darkened entry immediately adjacent to it, startling her.

"Welcome home, counselor," he said.

"Tony?" She stopped, her eyes searching the row of houses. "Is that you?"

Tony Alessandro—Anthony Salvatore Alessandro to the DMV, Detective Alessandro to his employer, the Philadelphia Police Department—stepped out of the shadowy entry of the house next to the Keyes' residence. The boy-next-door for all of Margo's childhood, Tony had grown up into one of the best looking men she'd ever known—classically handsome features that would be at home in a Roman temple; hair so dark it was almost black; brown eyes that could make her knees buckle with one look. A mouth that made kissing a sacrament.

He came down the steps with the easy grace of an athlete and met her at the end of the short walkway to his mother's house. Greeting her with a hug and a lingering kiss on the cheek he said, "It's been a long time since Mary Ellen's wedding last fall."

And there it was, the last thing making her nervous about this trip. Mary Ellen's wedding. When he'd danced with her all night before sneaking her out of the parish hall to a dark Sunday school classroom where he proceeded to kiss her senseless, making her mouth burn for his, her breasts ache for him to touch them and her whole body melt into a wet and wanting puddle. If his nephew hadn't dragged him away, she was sure they'd have ended up naked in his bed. Or on the floor of the classroom.

But she hadn't heard from him since.

She knew the blush that was the bane of her existence was now creeping up her neck but hoped the dusky light concealed it. "Yeah, you weren't around when I was here in April."

"I was in DC, meeting with this task force I'm on. I hear you're back for our class reunion."

"My mother's doing, not mine. She signed me up. The half-dozen people who emailed saying how great it was I would be there made me feel guilty enough that I didn't have the nerve to back out."

"Not like you to give in to social pressure."

"Maybe I'm getting soft in my old age."

"Better work on your argument, counselor. No one who's ever met you will believe that one." He'd kept his hand on her shoulder and was studying her face. "You look great. West Coast agrees with you, doesn't it?"

"It does. As much as Philly agrees with you. Every time I see you, I wonder if there's a portrait turning wrinkled, soft and flabby in an attic somewhere. I swear to God you still look like the guy the yearbook described. Let's see: best athlete in the class with the body to show for it. A smile that would melt glaciers. Brown eyes every girl wants to get lost in." She glanced over his broad shoulders and trim body in jeans and a denim jacket, and up at his handsome face. "Yup, all still there."

He dropped his arm, laughed and made a very Italian gesture, one that even a non-Italian, at least a non-Italian from Philadelphia, would recognize. "Jesus, Margo, leave it to you to remember that shit." He motioned toward her empty hands. "Not to change the subject but, no luggage? You're not staying with your mom?"

"Impressive analytic skills. No wonder you made detective on your first try. Congratulations on that, by the way. Where're you working?"

"Thanks. I'm working with the white-collar crime unit."

She looked embarrassed. "Good choice. You had a running start on the subject fifteen years ago, didn't you?"

"Are you evading my question about where you're staying, Madame Prosecutor? Can't imagine you let witnesses do something like that."

"No, sir, Detective Alessandro, I do not. I'm staying at the Bellevue. Between a conference in Center City next week and not wanting to go to the reunion feeling like the twelve-year-old I seem to turn into when I stay here, I thought it best."

"Sounds like neither one of us is too anxious to go to this thing." He looked away from her and stuck his hands in his jeans pockets.

"Why are you worried? I thought you went to all our class reunions."

"This time, Nicole will be there."

He didn't need to say more; she knew the story. Nicole, who'd been his off-again, on-again high school girlfriend and then fiancée, broke their engagement to elope with a much older—and definitely richer—man, banging up Tony's pride badly. Neighborhood gossip said it could only have been the promise of life on the prestigious Main Line that had won Nicole away from Tony. But then, the neighborhood always favored the Alessandro side of any story.

"I didn't think she did reunions, either."

"Not 'til this one."

"I hope you have a supermodel lined up to go with you."

"No date. You?"

"Surely the grapevine," she nodded toward their mothers' homes, "has already told you I don't." She pulled her gaze away from his and took a deep breath before blurting out, "Listen, not that I'm a supermodel, but I brought this fairly outrageous dress to wear with my new Manolo Blahniks. It might, I don't know, give our classmates something to talk about other than her if you arrive with the woman no one's seen in fifteen years, even if it is just me. And I wouldn't mind having company when I walk into that restaurant. It'd just be, you know, old friends…"

He held up his hand. "Slow down. So, you're volunteering to be my date?"

"I just think it might be advantageous for both of us if we went together."

"That sounds more like an offer to carpool."

"Really, just old friends doing each other a favor." She searched his face trying to anticipate his answer. "So…yes? No?"

"Now why would I turn down the chance to walk in with the class mystery woman in an outrageous dress and expensive shoes? Pick you up…when? "

"How about I pick you up? I don't think my new dress would fare well on your motorcycle."

"I'll bow to your transportation preferences. But the Bellevue's right around the corner from my apartment. I'll walk over so you won't have to look for a parking space."

"Great. Maybe come by at five and have a drink before we go so we can catch up?" The offer slipped out before she could think about it. "I'm in suite 832."

"I'll see you at five." He gave her a quick peck on the cheek. "Say hi to your mom for me."

At her mother's door, she dug around in her purse for the key, listening for the sound of Tony's cycle taking off so she could relax. Her mother opened the door before Margo could get it unlocked. "Hello, dear." She reached up and kissed her daughter. "Was that Anthony I heard?"

"Yes, Mom. He said to say hi."

Dolores Keyes' eyes lit up. "I'm glad you had a chance to talk with him. Did he say anything about the reunion? I hear he's going alone."

"He was, but we just made arrangements to go together."

"Oh, good." She pulled at her daughter's hand. "How silly to stand on the doorstep talking! I like your hair. It's a little longer than before, isn't it?" She closed the door after Margo. "Oh, and don't let me forget to give you the sticky buns I got for you."

The evening had begun the way visits with her mother always did—a comment about her hair and a bribe of sticky buns. It continued in its usual trajectory with Margo talking about Portland and her mother talking about friends and family in Philadelphia.

There was no mention of what had obsessed Margo every time she thought about this trip. But then they never discussed *that* subject.

In the fall of her senior year of high school, her father had been arrested on federal racketeering charges along with some of his clients, members of the Philly mob. All through that year, as one trial after another hit the headlines, Margo and her mother had dealt with the humiliation of learning that Kenny Keyes was not the kind of lawyer they thought he was. He'd been convicted and sent to federal prison. Dolores Keyes hadn't uttered his name since.

After they cleaned up the kitchen, Margo left, promising to join her mother and aunt the next day for lunch. But once at her hotel, she couldn't settle down. She tried convincing herself it was jet lag or maybe nervousness about seeing people she hadn't seen since high school. Eventually, she had to admit it was Tony keeping her awake.

Born a month apart to next-door neighbors, they'd been childhood playmates as well as high school classmates. His sisters were her best friends; she'd learned to dance with him when they were barely teenagers. He'd made sure she had fun down at the shore the summer after her father's trial. They hung out when she was back in Philly between college and law school. But somehow they never got beyond a close friendship, dinner-and-movie dates and some unforgettable kissing.

Maybe it was geography. They had spent most of the past fifteen years on opposite coasts, after all. Maybe they were never in the same place in their lives at the same time. Whatever it was, she'd always told herself settling for a warm, affectionate friendship was a good thing. After all, a relationship between a police officer and the daughter of a mob lawyer probably wasn't a match made in heaven.

Then his sister Mary Ellen got married.

In the mood for more Crimson Romance?
Check out *His Fantasy Maid*
by Susan Blexrud
at *CrimsonRomance.com*.